Portuguese Irregular Verbs

ALEXANDER McCALL SMITH

Portuguese
Irregular Verbs

Illustrations by
IAIN McINTOSH

Polygon

First published in Great Britain in 2003 by Polygon
an imprint of Birlinn Ltd
West Newington House
10 Newington Road
Edinburgh
www.birlinn.co.uk

Reprinted 2003

ISBN 0 9544075 6 3

British Library Cataloguing-in-Publication Data
A catalogue record is available on
request from the British Library.

Typeset by Antony Gray, London
Printed and bound by Creative Print & Design,
Ebbw Vale, Wales

This is for
REINHARD ZIMMERMANN

Contents

THE PRINCIPLES
OF TENNIS

PROFESSOR DR MORITZ-MARIA VON IGELFELD
often reflected on how fortunate he was to be exactly who he
was, and nobody else. When one paused to think of who one
might have been had the accident of birth not happened precisely
as it did, then, well, one could be quite frankly *appalled*. Take his
colleague Professor Dr Detlev Amadeus Unterholzer, for instance.
Firstly, there was the name: to be called Detlev was a misfortune,
but to add that ridiculous Mozartian pretension to it, and then to
culminate in Unterholzer was to gild a turnip. But if one then
considered Unterholzer's general circumstances, then Pelion was
surely piled upon Ossa. Unterholzer had the double misfortune of
coming from an obscure potato-growing area somewhere, a place
completely without consequence, and of being burdened in this
life with a large and inelegant nose. This, of course, was not
something for which he could be blamed, but one might certainly
criticise him, thought von Igelfeld, for carrying his nose in the way
he did. A difficult nose, which can afflict anybody, may be kept in
the background by a modest disposition of the head; Unterholzer,
by contrast, thrust his nose forward shamelessly, as might an ant-
eater, with the result that it was the first thing one saw when he

appeared anywhere. It was exactly the wrong thing to do if one had a nose like that.

The von Igelfeld nose, by contrast, was entirely appropriate. It was not small, but then a small nose is perhaps as much of a misfortune as a large nose, lending the wearer an appearance of pettiness or even irrelevance. Von Igelfeld's nose tended slightly to the aquiline, which was completely becoming for the scion of so distinguished a family. The von Igelfeld name was an honourable one: *Igel* meant hedgehog in German, and von Igelfeld, therefore, was *hedgehogfield*, an irreproachable territorial reference that was reflected in the family coat of arms – a hedgehog recumbent upon a background of vert. Unterholzer, of course, might snigger at the hedgehog, but what could he do but snigger, given that he had no armorial claims, whatever his pretensions in that direction might be.

But even if von Igelfeld was relieved that he was not Unterholzer, then he had to admit to himself that he would have been perfectly happy to have been Professor Dr Dr (*honoris causa*) Florianus Prinzel, another colleague at the Institute of Romance Philology. Prinzel was a fine man and a considerable scholar, whom von Igelfeld had met when they were both students, and whom he had long unconditionally admired. Prinzel was the athlete-poet; von Igelfeld the scholar – well, scholar-scholar one would probably have to say. If von Igelfeld had been asked to stipulate a Platonic von Igelfeld, an ideal template for all von Igelfelds, then he would have chosen Prinzel for this without the slightest hesitation.

Of the three professors, von Igelfeld was undoubtedly the most distinguished. He was the author of a seminal work on Romance philology, *Portuguese Irregular Verbs*, a work of such majesty that it dwarfed all other books in the field. It was a lengthy book of almost twelve hundred pages, and was the result of years of research into

the etymology and vagaries of Portuguese verbs. It had been well-received – not that there had ever been the slightest doubt about that – and indeed one reviewer had simply written, 'There is nothing more to be said on this subject. Nothing.' Von Igelfeld had taken this compliment in the spirit in which it had been intended, but there was in his view a great deal more to be said, largely by way of exposition of some of the more obscure or controversial points touched upon in the book, and for many years he continued to say it. This was mostly done at conferences, where von Igelfeld's papers on Portuguese irregular verbs were often the highlight of proceedings. Not that this eminence always bore the fruit that might be expected: unfortunately it was Prinzel, not von Igelfeld, who had received the honorary doctorate from the University of Palermo, and many people, including von Igelfeld, thought that this might be a case of mistaken identity. After all, from the viewpoint of the fairly diminutive Sicilian professors who bestowed the honour, three tall Germans might have been difficult to tell apart. These doubts, however, were never aired, as that would have been a breach of civility and a threat to the friendship. But just as the doubts were never mentioned, neither was the honorary doctorate.

At the Annual Congress of Romance Philology in Zürich, the three professors decided to stay in a small village on the edge of the lake. There was an excellent train which took them into the city each morning for the meeting, and in the evening they could even return by the regular boat, which called at the jetty no more than five minutes from the hotel. It was altogether a much more satisfactory arrangement than staying in Zürich itself, surrounded by banks and expensive watch shops. As von Igelfeld remarked to the others: 'Have you noticed how Zürich ticks? *Klummit, klummit, ding!* I could never sleep in such a town.'

The Hotel Carl-Gustav, in which the three professors stayed, was a large old-fashioned establishment, much favoured by families from Zürich who wanted to get away, but not too far away. Anxious bankers, into whose very bones the Swiss work ethic had penetrated, stayed there for their holidays. It was highly convenient for them, as they could tell their wives they were going for a walk in the hotel grounds and then slip off to the railway station and be in their offices in Zürich within twenty minutes. They could then return two hours later, to pretend that they had been in the woods or at the lakeside; whereas in reality they had been accepting deposits and discounting bills of exchange. In this way, certain Zürich financiers had acquired the reputation of never going on holiday at all, which filled their rivals with feelings of dread and guilt.

Prinzel had arrived first, and taken the best room, the one with the uninterrupted view of the lake. He had felt slightly uneasy about this, as it was a room which should really have gone to von Igelfeld, who always got the best of everything on the strength of *Portuguese Irregular Verbs.* For this reason Prinzel was careful not to mention the view and contrived to keep von Igelfeld out of his room so he could not see it for himself. Unterholzer, who always got the worst of what was on offer, had a slightly gloomy room at the side of the hotel, above the dining room, and his view was that of the hotel tennis court.

'I look out onto the tennis court,' he announced one evening as the three gathered for a glass of mineral water on the hotel terrace.

'Ah!' said von Igelfeld. 'And have you seen people playing on this tennis court?'

'I saw four Italian guests using it,' said Prinzel. 'They played a very energetic game until one of them appeared to have a heart attack and they stopped.'

The three professors contemplated this remarkable story for a few moments. Even here, in these perfect surroundings, where everything was so safe, so assured, mortality could not be kept at bay. The Swiss could guarantee everything, could co-ordinate anything – but ultimately mortality was no respecter of timetables.

Then Prinzel had an idea. Tennis did not look too difficult; the long summer evening stretched out before them, and the court, since the sudden departure of the Italians, was empty.

'We could, perhaps, have a game of tennis ourselves,' he suggested.

The others looked at him.

'I've never played,' said von Igelfeld.

'Nor I,' said Unterholzer. 'Chess, yes. Tennis, no.'

'But that's no reason not to play,' von Igelfeld added quickly. 'Tennis, like any activity, can be mastered if one knows the principles behind it. In that respect it must be like language. The understanding of simple rules produces an understanding of a language. What could be simpler?'

Unterholzer and Prinzel agreed, and Prinzel was despatched to speak to the manager of the hotel to find out whether tennis equipment, and a book of the rules of tennis, could be borrowed. The manager was somewhat surprised at the request for the book, but in an old hotel most things can be found and he eventually came up with an ancient dog-eared handbook from the games cupboard. This was *The Rules of Lawn Tennis* by Captain Geoffrey Pembleton BA (Cantab.), tennis Blue, sometime county champion of Cambridgeshire; and published in 1923, *before the tie-breaker was invented.*

Armed with Pembleton's treatise, described by von Igelfeld, to the amusement of the others, as 'this great work of Cambridge scholarship', the three professors strode confidently onto the court. Captain Pembleton had thoughtfully included several chapters describing tennis technique, and here all the major strokes were illustrated with little dotted diagrams showing the movement of the arms and the disposition of the body.

It took no more than ten minutes for von Igelfeld and Prinzel to feel sufficiently confident to begin a game. Unterholzer sat on a chair at the end of the net, and declared himself the umpire. The first service, naturally, was taken by von Igelfeld, who raised his racquet in the air as recommended by Captain Pembleton, and hit the ball in the direction of Prinzel.

The tennis service is not a simple matter, and unfortunately von Igelfeld did not manage to get any of his serves over the net. Everything was a double fault.

'Love 15; Love 30; Love 40; Game to Professor Dr Prinzel!' called out Unterholzer. 'Professor Dr Prinzel to serve!'

Prinzel, who had been waiting patiently to return von Igelfeld's serve, his feet positioned in exactly the way advised by Captain

Pembleton, now quickly consulted the book to refresh his memory. Then, throwing the tennis ball high into the air, he brought his racquet down with convincing force and drove the ball into the net. Undeterred, he tried again, and again after that, but the score remained obstinately one-sided.

'Love 15; Love 30; Love 40; Game to Professor Dr von Igelfeld!' Unterholzer intoned. 'Professor Dr von Igelfeld to serve!'

And so it continued, as the number of games mounted up. Neither player ever succeeded in winning a game other than by the default of the server. At several points the ball managed to get across the net, and on one or two occasions it was even returned; but this was never enough to result in the server's winning a game. Unterholzer continued to call out the score and attracted an occasional sharp glance from von Igelfeld, who eventually suggested that the *Rules of Tennis* be consulted to see who should win in such circumstances.

Unfortunately there appeared to be no answer. Captain Pembleton merely said that after six games had been won by one player this was a victory – provided that such a player was at least two games ahead of his opponent. If he was not in such a position, then the match must continue until such a lead was established. *The problem with this, though, was that von Igelfeld and Prinzel, never winning a service, could never be more than one game ahead of each other.*

This awkward, seemingly irresoluble difficulty seemed to all of them to be a gross flaw in the theoretical structure of the game.

'This is quite ridiculous,' snorted von Igelfeld. 'A game must have a winner – everybody knows that – and yet this . . . this *stupid* book makes no provision for *moderate* players like ourselves!'

'I agree,' said Prinzel, tossing down his racquet. 'Unterholzer, what about you?'

'I'm not interested in playing such a flawed game,' said Unterholzer, with a dismissive gesture towards *The Rules of Lawn Tennis.* 'So much for Cambridge!'

They trooped off the tennis court, not noticing the faces draw back rapidly from the windows. Rarely had the Hotel Carl-Gustav provided such entertainment for its guests.

'Well,' said Prinzel. 'I'm rather hot after all that sport. I could do with a swim.'

'A good idea,' said von Igelfeld. 'Perhaps we should do that.'

'Do you swim?' asked Unterholzer, rather surprised by the sudden burst of physical activity.

'Not in practice,' said von Igelfeld. 'But it has never looked difficult to me. One merely extends the arms in the appropriate motion and then retracts them, thereby propelling the body through the water.'

'That's quite correct,' said Prinzel. 'I've seen it done many times. In fact, this morning some of the other guests were doing it from the hotel jetty. We could borrow swimming costumes from the manager.'

'Then let's all go and swim,' said von Igelfeld, enthusiastically. 'Dinner's not for another hour or so, and it would refresh us all,' adding, with a glance at Unterholzer, 'players and otherwise.'

The waters were cool and inviting. Out on the lake, the elegant white yachts dipped their tall sails in the breeze from the mountains. From where they stood on the jetty, the three professors could, by craning their necks, see the point where Jung in his study had pondered our collective dreams. As von Igelfeld had pointed out, swimming was simple, in theory.

Inside the Hotel Carl-Gustav, the watching guests waited, breathless in their anticipation.

DUELS, AND HOW
TO FIGHT THEM

H EIDELBERG AND YOUTH! *Ach, die Jugendzeit!* When
he was a student, von Igelfeld lodged in Heidelberg with
Frau Ilse Krantzenhauf, a landlady of the old school. Her precise
age was a matter of speculation among generations of students, but
she showed no signs of retiring, and on their graduation from the
university her lodgers frequently promised to send their own sons
to her when the next generation's time came. For her part, Frau
Krantzenhauf solemnly promised to reserve a room for twenty or
so years hence. In many cases this promise was called upon, and a
fresh-faced boy from a Gymnasium in Hanover, or Hamburg, or
Regensburg would find himself received by his father's old landlady
and led to the very room which his father had occupied, to sit at the
same desk and look out at the same view.

Three other students lodged with Frau Krantzenhauf during
von Igelfeld's days in Heidelberg. Two of these were regarded by
von Igelfeld as being of no interest, and only barely to be tolerated.
Dorflinger was a tall, bony youth from a farm near Munich, while
Giesbach, his ponderous friend, was as rotund as Dorflinger was
thin. They both studied engineering, knew next to no Latin, and
spent every evening in a beer hall. Von Igelfeld exchanged a

few words with them and then retreated into silence. There was nothing more to say to people like that – nothing.

Far more congenial in von Igelfeld's view was a young student of philology from Freiburg, Florianus Prinzel. Prinzel was tall, had dark wavy hair, and invariably fixed those to whom he spoke with a direct, honest look. Von Igelfeld, whose notions of friendship were those of nineteenth-century romanticism, in which young men aspired to noble friendships, thought that here, at last, was one whose qualities he could respect. He, von Igelfeld, the aesthete-scholar, could befriend the athlete-hero, Prinzel. He could see it already; Prinzel streaking past his hopelessly outclassed competitors, leaping over hurdles, his brow high in the wind; Prinzel's manly chest breasting the finishing tape; Prinzel receiving the fencing trophy and handing it over to von Igelfeld to hold while he removed his gauntlets. It was to be the sort of friendship which had been commonplace fifty years before, in military academies and such places, but which had been irretrievably ruined by the reductionist insights of Vienna.

Unfortunately, von Igelfeld's vision of the relationship was fatally flawed. Although Prinzel was tall and strong, and perhaps should have been an athlete, he had not the slightest interest in athletic matters. Prinzel was, in fact, every bit as intellectual and bookish as was von Igelfeld, and not at all capable of being a hero on, or indeed off, the field. He could not run very fast; he had no interest in rowing; and he regarded ball games as absurd.

Undeterred, von Igelfeld decided that even if Prinzel were to prove slow to realise his natural prowess, he could be made to appreciate just how fundamentally he had mistaken his destiny. Von Igelfeld began to tell others of Prinzel's sporting instincts and abilities.

'My friend, Prinzel,' he would say, 'is very good at games. I'm not really so accomplished at that sort of thing myself, but you should see him. A consummate athlete!'

Others believed this, and soon Prinzel had a reputation of being a great sportsman. And if anybody thought it strange that they should never have seen Prinzel on the field, then they reasoned that this must be because he did not deign to do much with the very inferior competition which he found in Heidelberg.

'Is it true that Prinzel represented Germany somewhere at something or other?' von Igelfeld was asked from time to time.

'Yes, it's quite true,' he answered, not deliberately seeking to tell a lie, but replying in this way because he had persuaded himself that Prinzel must indeed be the holder of records of which he was silent. Or, if he were not the holder, then the records could certainly be his for the asking if only he would bother to win them.

It may all have remained at the level of fantasy, harmless enough, even if somewhat irritating for Prinzel, had it not been for von Igelfeld's sudden conviction that Prinzel could be a fine swordsman, were he to try the sport. Unprotected fencing amongst students was then strongly discouraged, even if there had been a time when it had flourished greatly in Heidelberg. In spite of this twentieth-century squeamishness, a small group of students obstinately adhered to the view that the possession of a small duelling scar on the cheek made an important statement about one's values, and was also of incidental value in later advancement in one's career. It was widely suspected that a man with a scar would always give a job to another man with a scar, even if there was a stronger, unscarred candidate. Of course, this mock duelling was carried out in a spirit of fun, and nobody was meant to be seriously hurt, but the flashing of swords and the graceful thrusts and parries of those unencumbered by clumsy protective jackets was much appreciated by the more reactionary students. These students were unexcited by the heady messages from Paris that made German universities in the nineteen-sixties and -seventies such hotbeds of radicalism and ferment.

The students who believed in fencing were naturally attracted to von Igelfeld. Not only was it his name that appealed to them, being redolent of an earlier era and lost territories, it was the knowledge of the estate in Austria and the close connection which von Igelfeld enjoyed with noble Bavarian families. For these reasons, von Igelfeld had been invited to take a glass of wine with the fencing faction.

The members of this group immediately realised that von Igelfeld, for all his background, was an unredeemed intellectual and therefore quite unsuited to any further involvement with their own, rather dark, social activities. At the same time, his background deserved respect and so they listened attentively to him as he spoke to them about his interest in the arid wastes of medieval Latin verse.

'And this Prinzel character,' one of them said. 'We see you about with him a great deal. Tell us something about him.'

'Prinzel's an amazing athlete,' von Igelfeld said. 'He's one of those people who's just naturally good at sports.'

This remark was met with silence. Several glances were exchanged.

'Is he a swordsman?' asked a rather heavily scarred young man, casually.

'He's a fine swordsman,' said von Igelfeld enthusiastically. 'In fact, I'm sure he'd be honoured to meet any of you gentlemen. At any time!'

Further glances were exchanged, unnoticed by von Igelfeld, who, draining his third glass of wine, was becoming slightly drunk.

'I'm most interested to hear that,' said the bearer of the scars. 'Could you tell him that I shall meet him next Friday evening at a place to be notified? Just for a bit of fun.'

'Of course,' said von Igelfeld, expansively. 'In fact, I can accept on his behalf, right now. We'll be there!'

Glasses were raised in a toast, and the conversation then moved on to the arrival in Heidelberg of two girls from Berlin whose interests were much to the taste of the group and whose company was being sought that Friday night, after the duel.

Prinzel was dismayed.

'You had no right to do that!' he protested, his voice raised in uncharacteristic anger. 'You had no right at all!'

Von Igelfeld gazed at his friend. So complete was his admiration for Prinzel, so utter his belief in the nobility of Prinzel's character, that he could not entertain the thought that the other might object to what was being proposed for him. It was as if he did not hear him.

'But it's all arranged,' went on von Igelfeld. 'And I shall be your second.' He added: 'That's the person who stands by, you know. He carries the towel.'

'For the blood?' snapped Prinzel. 'To mop up the blood?'

Von Igelfeld laughed dismissively. 'There's no need for blood,' he said. 'Blood hardly comes into it. You're not going to kill one another – this is merely a bit of sport!'

Prinzel waved his hands about in exasperation. 'I simply can't understand you,' he shouted. 'You seem to have a completely false notion of my character. I'm a scholar, do you understand? *I am not an athlete. I am not a hero.* I have absolutely no interest in fencing, none at all! I've never done it.'

Von Igelfeld appeared momentarily nonplussed.

'Never?' he said.

'Never!' cried Prinzel. 'Let me repeat myself. I am a scholar!'

Von Igelfeld now seemed to recover his composure.

'Scholars sometimes engage in martial pursuits,' he asserted. 'There are many precedents for this. And swordmanship is a traditional matter of honour at universities. We all know that. Why set your face against our heritage?'

Prinzel shook his head. For a few moments he was silent, as if at a loss for words. Then he spoke, in a voice which was weak with defeat.

'Who are these types?' he asked. 'How did you meet them?'

Noting his friend's tone of acceptance, von Igelfeld laid a hand on his shoulder, already the reassuring second.

'They are a group of very agreeable characters,' he said. 'They have some sort of *Korps*, in which they drink wine and talk about various matters. They asked to meet me because they thought I was old-fashioned.'

Von Igelfeld laughed at the absurdity of the notion. They would see next Friday just what sort of friends he had! Old-fashioned indeed!

Prinzel sighed.

'I suppose I have no alternative,' he said. 'You seem to have committed me.'

Von Igelfeld patted his friend's shoulder again.

'Don't you worry,' he said. 'It'll be a very exciting evening. You'll see.'

The place chosen for the match was a field which lay behind an inn on the outskirts of the city. The field was ringed by trees, which gave it a privacy which had been much appreciated by those who over the years had used it for clandestine purposes of one sort or another. When von Igelfeld and Prinzel arrived, they thought at first that there was nobody there, and for a brief joyous moment Prinzel imagined that the whole idea had been a joke played on von Igelfeld. This made him smile with relief, a reaction which von Igelfeld interpreted as one of confidence.

'Of course you're going to win,' he said excitedly. 'And afterwards we shall all have a grand celebration at the inn.'

Then, from out of the shadows, there stepped four members of the *Korps*. They looked perfectly sinister, clad in capes of some sort, with long suitcases in which the swords were concealed.

'Look, there they are!' shouted von Igelfeld excitedly. 'Hallo there, everybody! Here we are!'

Prinzel froze. Had von Igelfeld had the eyes to see, he would have been presented with a picture of a man facing a firing squad. Prinzel's face was white, his eyes wide with horror, his brow glistening with beads of sweat.

The scarred student stepped forward and shook von Igelfeld's hand. Then he crossed to Prinzel, bowed and introduced himself.

'This is a fine evening for sport,' he said. Gesturing to the weapons, he invited Prinzel to make his choice.

'We shall have six rounds of three minutes each,' said one of the *Korps*. 'When a gentleman draws blood, the contest shall stop.'

Von Igelfeld nodded eagerly.

'That's correct,' he said. 'That's how we do it.'

Prinzel glanced at his friend.

'How do you know?' he hissed angrily. 'If you know so much

about this, why don't you fight instead of me?'

'I fight?' said von Igelfeld, astonished. 'That's quite out of the question. I would lose, I'm afraid.'

Prinzel muttered something which von Igelfeld did not hear. It was too late now, anyway, as his opponent had now taken his position and everybody else was looking expectantly at Prinzel.

There was a flash of swords. Prinzel thrust forward and parried his opponent's strike. Then his own sword shot forward and steel met steel with a sharp metallic sound. Von Igelfeld gave a start.

Then it was stand-off again. Prinzel watched warily as his opponent began to move around him, sword raised almost to the lips, as if in salute. Then, so rapidly and daintily, as if to be invisible, the other's sword cut through the air with a whistling sound and, with almost surgical grace, sliced off the very tip of Prinzel's nose.

Prinzel stood quite still. Then, with a low moan, he dropped his sword and went down onto his hands and knees, as if searching for his severed flesh. For a few moments von Igelfeld was paralysed, unable to believe what he had seen. But then, remembering his duties as second, he shot forward, picked up the tip of the nose, a tiny, crumpled thing, and pressed it against his friend's face, as if to stick it back on.

Slowly Prinzel rose to his feet. There was not much blood – at least there was not as much as one might have expected – and he was able to maintain an aloof dignity.

'Take me to the hospital,' he said out of the corner of his mouth. 'And keep your hand where it is.'

Prinzel's opponent watched impassively.

'Well fought!' he said. 'You almost had me at the beginning.' Then, almost as an afterthought: 'Don't worry about that nick. It always seems so much worse than it really is. Imagine what a distinguished scar you will have! Bang in the middle of your face – can't be missed!'

The landlord of the inn called an ambulance, complaining all the while about the inconvenience to which students put him.

'They're always up to no good,' he grumbled, peering at Prinzel. 'I see you've been fencing. Would you believe it? This is the Federal Republic of Germany, you know, not Weimar. And we're meant to be in the second half of the twentieth century.'

Von Igelfeld looked at him scornfully.

'You don't even know what this is all about,' he said. 'It's a student matter; nothing to do with you. Nothing at all.'

[26]

It was Prinzel's misfortune to be attended at the hospital by a doctor who was drunk. Von Igelfeld thought that he could smell the fumes of whisky emanating from behind the surgical mask, but said nothing, reckoning it might be ether, or it might indeed be whisky, but used for medicinal purposes. Prinzel by now had closed his eyes, and was determined to hear, see and smell nothing. He felt von Igelfeld release the pressure on his face, and he felt the doctor's fumbling fingers. He felt a cold swab on his exposed arm, and then the prick of an injection. And after that, there was only numbness.

The drunken doctor examined the severed tip and realised that all that was required were several well-placed stitches. These he inserted rapidly. Then he stood back, admired his handiwork, and asked a nurse to apply a dressing. It had been a simple procedure, and there was no doubt but that the nose would heal up well within a few weeks. There would be a scar, of course, but that's what these young men wanted after all.

'You've made a very good recovery,' von Igelfeld said to Prinzel a fortnight later. 'You can hardly see the scar.'

Prinzel gazed at himself in the mirror. It was all very well for von Igelfeld to congratulate him on his recovery, but there was still something wrong. His nose looked different, somehow, although he could not decide exactly why this should be so.

Von Igelfeld had also studied Prinzel's nose and had come to a dreadful conclusion. The drunken doctor had sewn the tip on *upside down*. Of course he could not tell Prinzel that, as such knowledge could be devastating – to anyone.

'I shall remain silent,' thought von Igelfeld. 'In time he'll become accustomed to it, and that'll be the end of the matter.'

For Prinzel there was one consolation. Von Igelfeld no longer talked about his sporting prowess, and whenever references were made by others to such matters as fencing, or even noses, von Igelfeld immediately changed the subject.

EARLY IRISH
PORNOGRAPHY

IN THE FINAL YEARS OF his doctoral studies it had been von Igelfeld's dream to be invited to serve as assistant to one of the world's greatest authorities on Early Irish. This language, so complicated and arcane that there was considerable doubt as to whether anyone ever actually spoke it, had attracted the attention of German philologists from the late nineteenth century onwards. The great Professor Siegfried Ehrenwalt of Berlin, founder of the *Review of Celtic Philology*, had devoted his life to the reconstruction of the syntactical rules of the language, and he had been followed by a long line of philologists, the latest of whom was Professor Dr Dr Dr Dieter Vogelsang. It was with Vogelsang that von Igelfeld wished to work, and when the call at last came, he was overjoyed.

'I couldn't have hoped for a better start to my career,' he confided in Prinzel. 'Vogelsang knows more about past anterior verbs in Early Irish than anybody else in the world.'

'More than anyone in Ireland?' asked Prinzel dubiously. 'Surely they have their own institutes in Dublin?'

Von Igelfeld shook his head. 'Nobody in Ireland knows anything about Early Irish. This is a well-established fact.'

Prinzel was not convinced, but did not allow his doubt to diminish his friend's delight in his first post. He himself was still waiting. He had written to several institutes in Germany and Switzerland, but had received few encouraging replies. He could continue to study, of course, and complete another doctorate after the one on which he was currently engaged, but there would come a point at which without an assistantship he would seriously have to reconsider his academic career.

The post as assistant to Professor Dr Vogelsang involved a move to Munich. Von Igelfeld acquired lodgings in the house of Frau Elvira Hugendubel, the widow of the retired lawyer and dachshund breeder, Aloys Hugendubel. Dr Hugendubel had been the author of *Einführung in die Grundlagen des Bayerischen Bienenrechtes*, and Frau Hugendubel felt, as a result, that she was a part of the greater intellectual life. The presence of an academic lodger provided reassurance of this, as well as providing the widow with something to do.

Von Igelfeld settled happily into his new life. Each morning he would walk the three miles to Vogelsang's institute, arriving at exactly nine-fifteen and leaving in the evening at six o'clock. The hours in between were spent checking Vogelsang's references, searching out articles in the dustier corners of the library, and preparing tables of adjectives. It was the lowest form of work in the academic hierarchy, made all the more difficult by the tendency of Professor Vogelsang to publish papers based almost entirely on von Igelfeld's work, but under the Vogelsang name and with no mention made of von Igelfeld's contribution. In one case – which eventually prompted von Igelfeld to protest (in the gentlest, most indirect terms) – Vogelsang took a paper which von Igelfeld asked him to read and immediately published it under his *own name*. So brazen was this conduct that von Igelfeld felt moved to draw his superior's attention to the fact that he had been hoping to submit the paper to a learned journal himself.

'I can't see why you are objecting,' said Vogelsang haughtily. 'The paper will achieve a far wider readership under my name than under the name of an unknown. Surely these scholarly considerations are more important than mere personal vanity?'

As he often did, Vogelsang had managed to shift the grounds of argument to make von Igelfeld feel guilty for making a perfectly reasonable point. It was a technique which von Igelfeld had himself used on many occasions, but which he was to perfect in the year of his assistantship with Professor Vogelsang.

Frau Hugendubel, of course, provided copious amounts of sympathy.

'Young scholars have a difficult time,' she mused. 'Herr Dr Hugendubel never treated his young assistants with anything but the greatest courtesy. Herr Dr Hugendubel gave them books and encouraged them in every way. He was a very kind man.'

There were, of course, some benefits to which von Igelfeld was able to look forward. At the beginning of his assistantship, Vogelsang had alluded to a field trip to Ireland at some future date, and had implied that von Igelfeld could expect to accompany him. For some months, nothing more was said of this until the day when Vogelsang announced that they would be leaving in a fortnight's time and told von Igelfeld to arrange the tickets.

Frau Hugendubel insisted on packing von Igelfeld's suitcase herself. She starched his collars particularly carefully, folded his night-shirts and ironed the creases. A pile of freshly laundered handkerchiefs was tucked into a corner of the case and beside these she put a small jar of Bavarian honey for her lodger's breakfast toast.

They travelled by train to St Malo, where they caught the night steamer to Cork. Vogelsang and von Igelfeld had been allocated a shared cabin, an arrangement over which Vogelsang protested vociferously until von Igelfeld offered to sit up all night on the deck. By the time the coast of Ireland hove into sight through the morning mist, von Igelfeld was yawning and bleary-eyed; Vogelsang, fresh from his comfortable berth, greeted him cheerfully but berated him over his lack of enthusiasm for the sight of the Irish coast.

'Look,' he said. 'There, before us, is the blessed coast of Ireland, the island of saints. Can you not manage more than a yawn?'

They docked, and the German party made its way down the gangway of the steamer, into the welcoming arms of Dr Patrick Fitzcarron O'Leary, formerly of the Advanced Technical College, Limerick, and now Reader in Irish in the University College of Cork. He and Vogelsang knew one another well, and addressed one another as old friends. Then, turning to von Igelfeld, Vogelsang introduced his assistant.

'My assistant – Dr Moritz-Maria von Igelfeld.'

'Good heavens!' said Patrick Fitzcarron O'Leary opaquely, seizing von Igelfeld's hand. 'How are you then, Maria old chap?'

Von Igelfeld blanched. Maria? What a strange way to address somebody whom one had only just met. Did the Irish use the second Christian name in such circumstances? If that indeed was the custom, then how should he address O'Leary? Would it be rude to call him Dr O'Leary, which seemed the most correct thing to do?

For a few moments, von Igelfeld was utterly perplexed. So concerned was he to follow correct usage at all times, and in all places (even in Ireland), that it seemed appalling to him that he

[32]

should run the risk of committing a social solecism virtually the moment he set foot on Irish soil. He looked to Vogelsang for assistance, but his superior just stared back at him blandly, and then looked pointedly at the suitcases, which he was clearly expecting von Igelfeld to carry.

'Very well,' mumbled von Igelfeld. Adding, in his confusion, 'Not bad, in fact.'

'Good fellow,' said O'Leary. 'Absolutely. Good for you.'

O'Leary now seized both suitcases and led the visitors off to a somewhat battered car which he had parked up against the edge of the quay. Then, with von Igelfeld in the back seat and Vogelsang sitting beside the Irishman, they drove off erratically in the direction of the red-brick guest house in which the two visitors were to spend their first night in Ireland. It was all very strange to von Igelfeld, who had never before been further than France and Italy. Everything was so *here and there*; so well-loved and used; so lived-in. There were men with caps, standing on the street corners, doing nothing; there were women with jugs propped up in their doorways; there were orange cats prowling on the top of walls; churches with red walls and white marble lintels, and white religious statuary.

The next two days were spent largely in the company of O'Leary. He showed his visitors the university; he took them to lunch in hotels where the proprietors greeted him by name and appeared to make a great fuss of him; and he spent long hours locked in his study with Vogelsang – meetings to which von Igelfeld was not admitted. On these occasions, von Igelfeld walked through the streets of Cork, marvelling at the softness of the light on the warm brick buildings, sniffing at the heavy, languid air, savouring the feel of Ireland. Occasionally, small groups of boys followed him on these walks, calling out to the tall German in a language which von Igelfeld did not understand, but which he assumed to be the local dialect of English. Once, on a bridge, a woman threw a stone at him, and then crossed herself vigorously, but this occurrence did not trouble von Igelfeld in the slightest, as the stone missed, making a satisfactory plop in the water below.

That evening, O'Leary forsook Vogelsang, who wanted to retire early, and took von Igelfeld to a bar. It was a splendid, mirrored room, in which men in dark, shapeless suits leaned against the counter drinking black stout.

The barman greeted O'Leary with the same warmth that seemed to herald his every appearance in Cork.

'Now then, Paddy,' said the white-aproned tender. 'What is it this evening for you and your Teutonic friend over there.'

Paddy! thought von Igelfeld. That must be the name to use, and he replied to O'Leary's offer of a drink: 'A beer, if you don't mind, Paddy!'

The drinks poured, O'Leary guided von Igelfeld towards a section of the bar, where two of the men in dark suits were standing.

'Fitz, my friend,' said one of the men, slapping O'Leary on the back. 'Sure it's yourself, so it is!'

Fitz! thought von Igelfeld. Perhaps this was an alternative name which close friends used, just as his childhood friends had called him Morri, until they had put behind them the childish things. If that were the case, then he should avoid it, as its use would claim an intimacy which did not exist and the Irishman would think him rude. But just as this was resolved, the other man said:

'Pat, if it isn't you, then who is it?'

Von Igelfeld frowned. Here was another name – obviously a contraction of Patrick. That was plain enough, but what puzzled him was the choice of names. Was it an entirely free one? Could Pat become Paddy if one felt like it? Or could Fitzcarron become Fitz if a change seemed desirable? And what about O'Leary – was that ever used? He gazed down upon the white head to the glass of dark beer and wondered whether it was wise to leave the certainties of home. He had read that to travel is to expose oneself to all sorts of vulnerabilities, and surely this was true.

'Now then, von,' said O'Leary cheerfully. 'Tell me about yourself. You seem a fairly tall sort of person.'

The drinking companions nodded their heads in agreement, looking up at von Igelfeld with a mixture of awe and amusement.

'He is that,' said one, gravely. 'You're right there, O.'

Von Igelfeld put down his glass. O? Was that yet another contraction? Really, there was something very strange – and unsettling – about Ireland.

The two days in Cork ended with a trip to the railway station in O'Leary's old car and prolonged, emotional farewells on the platform. O'Leary slapped von Igelfeld on the back several times, to his considerable discomfort, while Vogelsang, with whom he had only shaken hands, looked on in undisguised amusement. Then their train drew out and they passed from the warm warren of red brick into the lush greenness of the countryside. Hedgerow-lined fields, low, folding hills; stone houses, white-washed, red-doored; lanes that wandered off into tight valleys; a blue curtain of sky that would without warning turn white, releasing sifting veils of rain; a sudden sight of children on a wall, tousle-haired, bare-legged, waving at the train; thus were they drawn deep into Ireland.

And then, in the distance, the hills appeared. The soft slopes merged into blue expanses, and the skies opened to wide canvases of cloud. The houses shrank, transformed themselves into clusters of tiny stone dwellings; and beyond was the sea, silver-blue, stretching out towards the pale, glowing horizon, and America.

'This is where Irish is spoken,' pronounced Vogelsang sacramentally. 'In these farmhouses, the verbs, the nouns, the differentiated adjectives – they're all still there.'

Von Igelfeld looked out of the window. Little droplets of rain coursed across the glass and made the countryside quiver. He had been thinking of how landscape moulds a language. It was impossible to imagine these hills giving forth anything but the soft syllables of Irish, just as only certain forms of German could be spoken on the high crags of Europe; or Dutch in the muddy, guttural, phlegmish lowlands. How sad it was that the language had been so largely lost; that it should survive only in these small pockets of the countryside. This was happening everywhere. The crudities of the modern world were simplifying or even destroying linguistic subtleties. Irregular verbs were becoming regular, the imperfect subjunctive was becoming the present subjunctive or, more frequently, disappearing altogether. Where previously there might have been four adjectives to describe a favoured hill, or the scent of new-mown hay, or the action of threading the warp of a loom, now there would only be one, or none. And as we lost the words, von Igelfeld thought, we lost the texture of the world that went with them.

It was at this moment, as the train drew into the small, apparently deserted station at which the two passengers were due to alight, that von Igelfeld realised what his life's work would be. He would do everything in his power to stop the process of linguistic debasement, and he would pick, as his target, the irregular verb. This moment, then, was the germ of that great work, *Portuguese Irregular Verbs*.

The station was not deserted. An ancient station master, surprised at the arrival of passengers, emerged from a green wooden building and agreed to take them to the small hotel which was to be found at the nearby loughside. There they settled in, the only guests, and ate a meal, while a succession of people passed by the dining room window, affecting nonchalance, and then staring in hard at the two Germans.

The next day was the first working day of the field trip. Vogelsang had been told of the existence of an extremely old man who lived on a nearby hillside and who spoke a version of Irish which was considered by all to be exceptionally archaic. If there were to be any vestiges of Old Irish extant, then in the words used by this old man might such linguistic remnants be found.

'You can certainly call on old Sean,' said the hotel proprietor. 'But I can't guarantee your reception. He may speak interesting Irish, but he's an extremely unpleasant, smelly old man. Not even the priest dares go up there, and that's saying something in these parts.'

Undaunted, Vogelsang led the way up the narrow, unused track that led to Sean's cottage. At last they reached it and, carefully negotiating the ramble of surrounding pig-sties, they approached the front door.

Vogelsang knocked loudly, and then called out (in Old Irish): 'We are here, Sean. I am Professor Vogelsang from Germany. And this young man is my assistant.'

There was silence from within the cottage. Vogelsang knocked again, louder now, and this time elicited a response. A frowning, weather-beaten face, caked with dirt, appeared at the window and gesticulated in an unfriendly fashion. Vogelsang bent down and put his face close to the window so that his nose was barely a few inches from Sean, but separated by a pane of clouded glass.

[37]

'Good morning, Sean,' said Vogelsang. 'We have come to talk to you.'

Sean appeared enraged. Shouting now, he hurled words out at the visiting philologists, shaking both fists in Vogelsang's face.

'Quick,' said Vogelsang, momentarily turning to von Igelfeld. 'Transcribe everything he says. Do it phonetically.'

As Sean continued to hurl abuse at Vogelsang, von Igelfeld's pencil moved swiftly over the paper, noting everything that the cantankerous and malodorous farmer said. Vogelsang nodded all the while, hoping to encourage the Irishman to open the door, but only succeeding in further annoying him. At last, after almost three quarters of an hour, Vogelsang observed that the visit might come to an end, and with the echoing shouts of Sean following them down the hill, they returned to the hotel.

A further attempt to visit Sean was made the next day, and the day after that, but the visitors were never admitted. They did, however, collect a full volume of transcribed notes on what he shouted at them through the door, and this was analysed each evening by a delighted Vogelsang.

'There is some very rare material here,' he said, poring over von Igelfeld's phonetic notations. 'Look, that verb over there, which is used only when addressing a pig, was thought to have disappeared centuries ago.'

'And he used it when addressing us?' said von Igelfeld wryly.

'Of course,' snapped Vogelsang. 'Everything he says to us is, in fact, obscene. Everything you have recorded here is a swear word of the most vulgar nature. But very old. Very, very old!'

They spent a final day in the hotel, this time not attempting to visit Sean, but each engaging in whatever pursuit he wished. Von

Igelfeld chose to explore the paths that wound around the lough. He took with him a sandwich lunch prepared for him by the hotel, and spent a contented day looking at the hills and watching the flights of water birds that rose out of the reeds on his approach. He met nobody until, at the very end of the day, he encountered Vogelsang coming in the opposite direction. Vogelsang looked furtive, as if he had been caught doing something illicit, and greeted von Igelfeld curtly and correctly, as one might greet a slight acquaintance on the street of a busy town. Von Igelfeld began to tell him of the wild swans he had seen: 'Four and twenty were there,' he began; but Vogelsang ignored him and he stopped.

The next day they returned to the railway station and boarded the train back to Cork. The mountains were now behind them, shrinking into a haze of blue. Von Igelfeld looked back wistfully, knowing, somehow, that he would never return. In Cork they only had a few hours to pass before the steamer sailed. These hours were filled by Patrick Fitzcarron O'Leary, who materialised from the railway station bar and was soon locked in earnest discussion with Vogelsang over the lists of words which had been obtained.

It was dark by the time they boarded the steamer. After they had been shown their cabins (to von Igelfeld's relief he had been allocated a berth) they both stood at the railings and looked down on the quay. It was raining, but only with that light, warm drizzle that seems always to embrace Ireland, and it did not deter them from standing bare-headed in the dampness. O'Leary had taken up position under the shelter of a crane, and he waved to them as the boat edged out from the quay. He continued to wave until they were out of the harbour, when he extracted a torch from his pocket and waved that. That was the last they saw of Ireland, a tiny pin-prick of light moving in the darkness, winking at them.

Back in Munich, von Igelfeld was greeted warmly by Frau Hugendubel and shown up to his spotlessly clean room. When she withdrew, he unpacked his suitcase, noticing the jar of honey, which he had not touched. This he put on a shelf for future use. Then he sat down and spread out on his desk the lists of words which he had transcribed during their encounters with Sean. Vogelsang wanted them arranged alphabetically and tabulated, with approximate German translations written opposite. Von Igelfeld began his task.

After an hour of work, von Igelfeld felt the desire to go out and have a cup of coffee in his favourite café nearby. He would buy a newspaper, read the Munich news, and then get back to his desk for further work. It would be a way of returning to Germany; his head, he feared, was still full of Ireland. He slipped out and walked briskly to the café.

A short time later, his half-read newspaper under his arm, he returned to the house and made his way upstairs. His door was open, and Frau Hugendubel stood in his room, be-aproned, clutching a feather duster.

'Dr von Igelfeld,' she said, her voice shaking with emotion. 'I must ask you to leave this house immediately.'

Von Igelfeld was astonished.

'To leave?' he stuttered. 'Do you mean to move out?'

Frau Hugendubel nodded.

'I would never have known you to be a . . . ' she paused. 'A pornographer!'

Von Igelfeld saw her throw a frightened glance towards his desk and he knew at once what it was all about.

'Oh that!' he laughed. 'Those words . . . '

Frau Hugendubel cut him short.

'I do not wish to exchange one more word with you,' she said, her voice firmer now. 'I shall not ask you for the rent you owe me, but I shall be grateful if you vacate the room within two hours.'

She cast a further disappointed glance into the room, this time at the jar of unopened honey, and then, shuddering her way past her deeply-wronged lodger, she disappeared down the stairs.

When he heard the next day of the misunderstanding and of von Igelfeld's plight, Vogelsang declined to intervene.

'It's most unfortunate,' he said. 'But there's nothing I can do. You should not have left obscene words on your desk.'

Von Igelfeld stared at Vogelsang. He knew now that Irish philology was a mistake and that it was time to move on. He would find another professor who would take him on as assistant, and his career would be launched afresh. Enquiries were made and letters were written, leading, at last, to an invitation from Professor Walter Schoeffer-Henschel to join him as his second assistant at the University of Wiesbaden. This was exactly what von Igelfeld wanted, and he accepted with alacrity. The air was filled with the scent of new possibilities.

ITALIAN MATTERS

TEN YEARS PASSED – JUST LIKE THAT – *pouf!* By the time he was thirty-five, after a long period in the service of Schoeffer-Henschel, von Igelfeld had received a call to a chair and was safely established in the Institute. In the years that followed, and particularly after the publication of that great work, *Portuguese Irregular Verbs*, honour upon honour fell upon von Igelfeld's shoulders. These brought the rewards of recognition – the sense of *value* of one's work and the knowledge of pre-eminence in the subject. And it also brought frequent invitations to conferences, all of which seemed to be held in most agreeable places, often, to von Igelfeld's great pleasure, in Italy.

It had been a tedious day at the Comparative Philology Conference in Siena. Professor Alberto Morati, the host, had given his paper on Etruscan pronouns – for the fourth time. Many of the delegates were familiar with it: von Igelfeld had heard it before in Messina five years previously. He had then heard it again in Rome the following year, and had caught the very end of its final section in Montpelier. Prinzel had heard it too, in his case in Buenos Aires, and had found the pace of the argument and its ponderous conclusions quite soporific, even in such an exotic location.

But even if Morati were not enough, the chairman of the conference had called on that legend of the international philology network, Professor J. G. K. L. Singh, of Chandighar. As the great Indian philologist (author of *Terms of Ritual Abuse in the Creditor/ Debtor Relationship in Village India*) ascended the platform, there emanated from the audience a strange sound; an inspiration of breath or a spontaneous communal sigh – it was difficult to tell which. Those delegates nearest the door were able to creep out without too much disturbance; those closer to the platform were trapped. Amongst the escapees was von Igelfeld, who spent the next two hours in the Cathedral Museum, admiring the illuminated manuscripts. Von Igelfeld then had time to take a cup of scalding, strong coffee in a nearby bar, read the front two pages of *Corriere della Sera*, and post three letters at the post office before returning to face the last five minutes of Professor J. G. K. L. Singh.

'Do not underestimate the extent of the problem,' Singh warned the delegates. 'The usage of the verb prefix "ur-rachi" (sometimes represented as "ur-rasti" is not necessarily indicative of a close relationship between addressor and addressee. *In fact, quite the opposite may be the case.* Just as a Frenchman might say to one who assumes excessive familiarity in modes of address: "Don't you *tutoyer* me", so too might one who wishes to maintain his distance say: "Don't you 'ur-rachi' me, if you ('ur-rachi') please!" In so doing, however, he might himself use the "ur-rachi" form, thus loading his own prohibition with deep irony, even sarcasm.'

Professor J. G. K. L. Singh continued in this fashion for a short time further and then, to enthusiastic applause from his relieved audience, left the platform. This was the signal for von Igelfeld to ask his question. It was the same question which he had asked Professor J. G. K. L. Singh before, but von Igelfeld could think of

[44]

no other, and the delegates relied on him to save them all the embarrassment of nothing being said.

'Is it the case, Professor J. G. K. L. Singh,' asked von Igelfeld, 'that the imperfect subjunctive has no insulting connotations in India?'

'Not at all!' said J. G. K. L. Singh, indignantly. 'I can't imagine who told you that! It is quite possible to give an imperfect subjunctive insult in Hindi. There are countless examples.'

So the debate continued. Professor Hurgert Hilpur of Finland delivered his paper, and was replied to by Professor Verloren van Themaat (Amsterdam); Professor Verloren van Themaat then gave his own paper, and was replied to by Professor Hurgert Hilpur. Professor Dr Dr Florianus Prinzel asked a question, which was answered by Professor Alberto Morati, who was contradicted, with some force, by Dr Domenico Palumbieri (Naples). There were many treats.

At the final session of the conference, von Igelfeld announced to Prinzel and Unterholzer that he proposed to visit Montalcino, a village in the Sienese hills, renowned for its Brunello wine and for the subtle beauty of the surrounding countryside. His suggestion enthused the other two, but as they were committed on the Friday and the Saturday, they would be able to join him there only on Sunday afternoon.

'I shall go first then,' said von Igelfeld. 'By the time you arrive on Sunday I shall have identified all the principal sights and shall be able to conduct you to them personally.'

Prinzel and Unterholzer thought this a good idea, and so late on the Friday morning they escorted von Igelfeld to the bus station near the Church of Santa Caterina and duly despatched him. In little more than an hour, von Igelfeld's blue-grey bus was climbing up the steep, winding road that led to Montalcino. At the small Church of Santa Maria he disembarked, glanced over the low wall at the countryside so far below, and walked the few yards to the Albergo Basilio, of which he had read in his guide to the hotels of Tuscany. The guide said very little, but ended its entry with the curious remark: *Caution advised, if you are German.*

The Albergo Basilio was a small, intimate country inn, of the sort which has so largely died out in all but the most remote corners of Europe. It had no more than ten beds, in plain, white-washed rooms; a parlour with a few chairs and a glass-topped table; and a dining room that gave off the kitchen. Its charm undoubtedly lay in its simplicity. There were no telephones, no artificial comforts; nothing, in fact, which would not be found in a modest farmhouse.

The owner was Signora Margarita Cossi, the widow of a raisin merchant from Grosseto. She had bought the hotel cheaply from her husband's cousin, and had made a moderate success of the enterprise. The hotel was well-placed to do considerably better than that, of course; Montalcino drew many wine pilgrims, and one might have expected the hotel to be full all the time. Unfortunately, this was not the case, and many visitors avoided staying there for more than one night and even went so far as to warn their friends against it. And the reason for this, beyond doubt, was the rudeness of Signora Cossi, who was an incorrigible xenophobe. She disliked people from Rome; she detested Venetians; she despised anybody from the South, and her views on the other nations of Europe were cussedly uncomplimentary. About every nation she had a deep-rooted prejudice, and when it came to the Germans this took the form of the conviction that they ate better, and in larger quantities, than any other people in Europe.

[46]

The source of this prejudice was a magazine article which Signora Cossi had read in an old issue of *Casa Moderna*, in which the author had disclosed to the readers that the average German was fifteen pounds overweight. Signora Cossi was so horrified by this figure, that it was but a short step to the conclusion that the quantities of food which they must have eaten to achieve this impressive obesity could only have been obtained at the expense of less gluttonous nations, particularly the Italians. On this basis, Signora Cossi took to making disparaging remarks about her German guests and making them feel unwelcome.

Von Igelfeld had no inkling of what lay ahead when he signed the register and handed over his passport to Signora Cossi that morning.

'I hope that you are comfortable here,' she said, glancing at his passport, 'Signor von Whatever. I know you people like your physical comfort.'

Von Igelfeld laughed. 'I'm sure that I shall be well looked after,' he assured her. 'This hotel seems delightful.'

'You've hardly seen it,' said Signora Cossi dismissively. 'Do you always make your mind up so quickly?'

Von Igelfeld gave a polite, if somewhat forced smile. 'Yes,' he said. 'When a place is so clearly delightful as this is, I see no point in prevarication.'

Signora Cossi looked at him suspiciously, but said nothing more. Silently she handed him his key and pointed to the stairway that led to the bedrooms. Von Igelfeld took the proffered key, bowed slightly, and went off up the stairs with his suitcase. He was unsure whether he had inadvertently said something offensive and whether Signora Cossi had the right to be so short with him. Had he used an unusually familiar term? He thought of

[47]

Professor J. G. K. L. Singh and his 'ur-rachis'. Had he unwittingly 'ur-rachied' this disagreeable woman?

Although he did not yet realise it, von Igelfeld had been allocated the worst room in the hotel. There was no furniture in it at all apart from a single bed, covered with a threadbare cotton cover. This bed had been bought second-hand from the house of a deceased dwarf in Sant'Amato, and was therefore very short. Von Igelfeld gazed at it in disbelief and then, putting down his suitcase, tried to lie down on the bed. He put his head on the pillow and then hoisted his legs up, but the bed was a good thirty inches too short and his calves, ankles and feet hung down over the edge. It would be impossible to sleep in such a position.

After a few minutes of uncomfortable meditation, von Igelfeld made his way downstairs again. Signora Cossi was still at her desk, and she watched him with narrowed eyes as he came down into the hall.

'Is everything all right?' she asked. Her tone was not solicitous.

'The room itself is charming,' said von Igelfeld courteously. 'But I'm afraid that I find the bed somewhat short for my needs.'

Signora Cossi's eyes flashed.

'And what might these needs be?' she challenged. 'What are you proposing to do in that bed?'

Von Igelfeld gasped.

'Nothing,' he said. 'Nothing at all. It is just that my legs do not fit. The bed is too short for me to lie down upon. That's all.'

Signora Cossi was not to be so easily placated.

'It's a perfectly good Italian bed,' she snapped. 'Are you suggesting that Italians are shorter than . . . than others?'

Von Igelfeld held up his hands in a gesture of horrified denial.

'Of course not,' he said quickly. 'I suggest no such thing. I'm sure I shall sleep very well after all.'

Signora Cossi appeared to subside somewhat.

'Dinner,' she said grudgingly, 'will be served at seven o'clock. Sharp.'

Von Igelfeld thanked her, handed over his key, and set off for his afternoon walk. There were many paths to be explored; paths that went up and down the hillside, through olive groves, vineyards, and forests of cypress. There was much to be seen before Prinzel and Unterholzer arrived, and he was determined to be as familiar as possible with the surroundings before Sunday. In that way he would have a psychological advantage over them which could last for the rest of the Italian trip, and even beyond.

Outside, the air was pleasantly cool. Von Igelfeld thought of how hot it would be in Siena, and how uncomfortable Prinzel and Unterholzer would be feeling. The thought set him in good humour for his walk, although the problem of his bed remained niggling in the back of his mind. It was not true what Signora Cossi had said: Italian beds were by no means all that size. His bed in the Hotel del Palio in Siena had been of generous proportions, and he had encountered no difficulty in sleeping very well in it. Of course, it might be that people in hill towns were naturally shorter – there were such places, particularly in Sicily, where sheer, grinding poverty over the generations had stunted people, but surely not in Tuscany.

Von Igelfeld looked about him for confirmation. There were not many people out in the narrow street that led to the Pineta, but those who were about seemed to be of average height. There was a stout priest, sitting on a stone bench, reading a sporting newspaper; there was a woman standing in her doorway peeling potatoes; there were several boys in the small piazza at the end of the road, taunting and throwing stones at the goldfish in the ornamental pond. If this were a representative selection of the population, there was nothing unusually small about them.

Von Igelfeld was puzzled. There was definitely something abnormal about the bed, and he decided to take it up with the hotel on his return. He began to suspect that it might be some sort of calculated insult. He had experienced this once before at a conference in Hamburg, when a socialist waiter, who no doubt harboured a bone-deep resentment of all *vons*, had deliberately placed his thumb (with its dirt-blackened nail) in his soup.

He reached the Pineta, the small municipal park on the edge of the town. He admired the pines and then struck off along the road that led to Sant'Angelo in Colle. Soon he was in the deep country-side, making his way along a dusty white track that led off to the west. Classical Tuscan vistas now opened up on both sides of him; hills, valleys, red-roofed farmhouses, oaks, somnolent groves. He passed a farmyard with its large, stuccoed barn and a cluster of trees under which rested an ancient wooden-wheeled cart. A man came out of the house, waved a greeting to von Igelfeld, and then disappeared into the barn. A few moments later he re-emerged, herding before him two great white oxen with floppy ears and giant horns. Von Igelfeld smiled to himself. This was the real Italy, unchanged since the days of Virgil. This might be Horace's farm; the farmer himself a pensioned poet, like Horace, perhaps, tired of the high culture of the city, now seeking the solace of rustic life.

Von Igelfeld's walk continued for some miles more. Then, as evening approached, he turned and made his way back to Montalcino. By the time he reached the Albergo Basilio it was already dusk, and the lights were on in the streets and in the piazza. He retrieved his key, ventured under the shower in the small bathroom off his room (he was unable to persuade the hot tap to work) and then, refreshed and more formally dressed, he made his way downstairs for dinner.

There were three other guests in the dining room, and all three responded courteously to von Igelfeld's murmured greeting. Von Igelfeld sat down at a table near the window, and picked up the small hand-written menu. There was not a great deal of choice: soup or mozzarella; pasta; lamb cutlet or stew; ice cream or cake. Von Igelfeld pondered: rural soups could be strong and rich – perhaps that was the delicious smell he had noticed as he came downstairs. He would start, then, with soup and proceed to the lamb cutlets by way of a bowl of pasta. He had walked a considerable distance that day, and he felt justifiably hungry. He would also order half a bottle of Brunello, which may well have come from one of the vineyards he had seen on his walk.

It was a full ten minutes before Signora Cossi appeared and stood before von Igelfeld, pencil poised to take his order for dinner.

'The cooking smells delicious,' said von Igelfeld politely. 'I am looking forward to my meal.'

'Oh yes, I'm sure you are,' said Signora Cossi. 'You Germans certainly enjoy your meals. You polish off most of Europe's food anyway.'

Von Igelfeld's mouth dropped open in surprise. He was utterly flabbergasted by the accusation and for a few moments he was quite unable to reply.

'Not that I blame you,' went on Signora Cossi, staring pointedly out of the window. 'If you can afford it, eat it, I always say. And that's certainly what you people do, even if it means short rations for the rest of us.'

Von Igelfeld looked away. Really, this woman was impossible! He had never been so profoundly insulted in his life, and he was tempted to rise to his feet and walk out without further ceremony. But something stopped him. No. That would just play into her hands. Instead, he would show her.

'You are quite wrong,' he said. 'In fact, I was just about to ask you whether you had something lighter – a salad perhaps.'

Signora Cossi curled a lip, clearly annoyed.

'Is that all?' she asked abruptly.

'Yes, please,' said von Igelfeld. 'A small mixed salad is all I require.'

'And to drink?' said Signora Cossi. 'A bottle of Brunello?'

'No thank you,' said von Igelfeld, through pursed lips. 'Water, please.'

'With gas?' Signora Cossi's pencil hovered above her pad.

'No,' said von Igelfeld firmly. He would deny himself even that. He would show her. 'Without.'

That night passed in agony. Hungry and uncomfortable, von Igelfeld tried every possible way of arranging his frame on the tiny bed, but was unable to prevent his legs from hanging painfully over the edge. Eventually, by placing a chair at the end and putting his pillow on it, he managed to create an extension to the bed. Although his head and neck were now uncomfortable, he at last dropped off to sleep.

The night was plagued with bad dreams. In one, he was walking through the Pineta, admiring the pine trees, when he suddenly came upon Professor J.G.K.L. Singh. The Indian philologist was delighted to see him, and insisted on raising a hopelessly abstruse point. Von Igelfeld awoke, sweating, cramped and uncomfortable. After a time he drifted off to sleep again, but only to encounter Signora Cossi in his dreams. She looked at him balefully, as if

accusing him of some unspoken wrong, and again he awoke, feeling unsettled and vaguely guilty.

The next morning, von Igelfeld went down for breakfast and found a single, frugal roll on his plate. Signora Cossi arrived to give him coffee and asked him whether he would like another roll. Von Igelfeld was about to order three, when he remembered his resolve of the previous evening and checked himself. Signora Cossi, looking somewhat disappointed, walked away to deal with another guest.

After breakfast, von Igelfeld walked out into the village. He bought *La Nazione* from the small paper shop and began to walk down the street, glancing at the headlines. Everything in Italy was coming apart, the newspaper said. The Government was tottering, the currency unsteady. The judiciary and the courts were being held to ransom by organised criminals from Naples and Palermo; there were daily kidnaps and every sort of atrocity. And now, as if to confirm the country's humiliation, the Japanese were buying up all of Italy's small-denomination coins and taking them off to Japan to make into buttons! It was infamous. He would read about all this in the piazza, and then set off to inspect the Church of Saint Joseph the Epistulist, to be found in a neighbouring hamlet.

He turned a corner in the street and found himself outside a small grocer's shop. In the window were loaves of bread, cakes, and thick bars of chocolate. The Italian State might be crumbling, but it would not stop the Italians enjoying pastries and chocolate. Von Igelfeld stopped, and stared at the food. Several cups of coffee had taken the edge off his appetite, but his hunger was still there in the background. And later it would be worse, after his walk, and he would never be able to order a decent meal from the dreadful Signora Cossi.

Von Igelfeld entered the shop. He was the only customer, and the woman who owned the shop appeared to be talking on the telephone in a back room. Von Igelfeld looked at the shelves, which were packed with household provisions of every sort. His eye fell on a packet of almond biscuits and then on a large fruit tart; both of these would do well. He could eat the fruit tart while sitting in the Pineta, and the almond biscuits would do for the walk itself.

The woman put down the telephone and emerged, smiling, into the shop. At that moment, the door from the street opened and in came Signora Cossi.

'*Buongiorno dottore*,' said the shopkeeper to von Igelfeld. 'What can I do for you this morning?'

Von Igelfeld froze, aware of the penetrating stare of Signora Cossi behind him.

'Do you have a pair of black shoe-laces?' he asked.

The shopkeeper reached for a box behind her and von Igelfeld

[54]

bought the laces. Signora Cossi said nothing, but nodded curtly to him as he left the shop. Once outside, von Igelfeld bit his lip in anger.

'I shall not be intimidated by that frightful woman,' he muttered to himself. 'I shall make her eat her words.'

He strode off, tossing the shoe-laces into a rubbish bin. Ahead of him lay a long walk, fuelled only by hunger. He thought of Prinzel and Unterholzer. They would no doubt be sitting in some outdoor cafe in Siena, enjoying coffee and cakes. Unterholzer, in particular, had a weakness for cakes; von Igelfeld had seen him on one occasion eat four at one sitting. That was the sort of gluttony which gave Germany a bad name. It was Unterholzer's fault.

That evening, von Igelfeld again returned from the walk shortly before dinner. The menu was unchanged, and the smell of the soup was as delicious as before. But again, he ordered a small helping of salad and two slices of thin bread. This time, Signora Cossi tried to tempt him by listing the attractions of the lamb cutlets.

'Thank you, but no,' said von Igelfeld airily. 'I do not eat a great deal, you know. There is far too much emphasis on food in Italy, I find.'

He tossed the comment off lightly, as one would throw in a pleasantry, but it found its target. Signora Cossi glared at him, before turning on her heels and marching back into the kitchen. Von Igelfeld's salad, when it arrived twenty-five minutes later, was smaller than last night, being composed of one tomato, four small lettuce leaves, two slices of cucumber and a shaving of green pepper. The bread, too, was so thinly sliced that through it von Igelfeld was able to read the inscription *Albergo Basilio* on the plate.

Another night of physical agony passed. At least this evening there were no dreams of Professor J. G. K .L. Singh, but as he lay on his sleepless and uncomfortable couch, von Igelfeld thought of what he could say to Signora Cossi when he at last left on Monday morning. Prinzel and Unterholzer were due to arrive at three the following afternoon, and to spend a night in the hotel before they all left for Florence. He would tell them about her insults, and they might be able to suggest suitable retorts. It would be easier, perhaps, when they outnumbered her.

The next day, Sunday, von Igelfeld refused his roll at breakfast and merely drank three cups of coffee. This will show her, he thought grimly; even if she failed to abandon her prejudice after this, she could surely take no pleasure in it. There must, after all, be a limit to the extent of self-deception which people can practise.

He left the hotel at half past ten and set off along the route he had followed on his first walk. By noon he found himself approaching the farm which had so entranced him before, and he saw, to his pleasure, that the farmer was busy unyoking the two large oxen from his cart. Von Igelfeld left the road and offered to help with the harnesses. His offer was gratefully received, and afterwards the farmer, pleased to discover that von Igelfeld spoke Italian, introduced himself and invited von Igelfeld to take a glass of wine with him and his wife.

They sat at a table under one of the oak trees, a flask of home-produced wine before them. Toasts were exchanged, and von Igelfeld closed his eyes with pleasure as the delicious red liquid ran down his parched throat. Glasses were refilled, and it was when these had been emptied that the farmer's wife invited von Igelfeld to stay for lunch.

'My wife is one of the best cooks in Tuscany,' said the farmer, bright-eyed. 'That's why I married her.'

'I should not wish to impose,' said von Igelfeld, hardly daring to believe his good fortune.

'It would be no imposition at all,' he was reassured by the farmer's wife. 'We have so much food here, and only two mouths to eat it now that our children have gone to Milan. You would be doing us a favour, truly you would.'

The meal was served at the table under the tree. To begin with they ate *zuppa crema di piselli*, rich and delicious. This was followed by bowls of *tagliatelle alla paesana*, heavy with garlic. Finally, an immense casserole dish of *capretto al vino bianco* was brought out, and of this everybody had three helpings.

Von Igelfeld sat back, quite replete. During the meal, conversation had been somewhat inhibited by the amount of food which required to be consumed, but now it picked up again.

'You must be a happy man,' observed von Igelfeld. 'How lucky you are to live here, in this charming place. It's so utterly peaceful.'

The farmer nodded.

'I know,' he said. 'I've never been to Rome. I've never even set foot in Florence, if it comes to that.'

'Nor Siena,' interjected his wife. 'In fact, you've never been anywhere at all.'

The farmer nodded. 'I don't mind: enough happens here to keep us busy.'

'Oh it does,' agreed his wife. 'Tell the *professore* about the angels.'

The farmer glanced at von Igelfeld.

'We have seen angels here,' he said quietly. 'On several occasions. Once, indeed, while we were sitting under this very tree. Two of them passed more or less overhead and then vanished behind those hills over there.'

Von Igelfeld looked up into the echoing, empty sky. It seemed quite possible that angels might be encountered in such a setting. It was against such landscapes, after all, that Italian artists had painted heavenly flights; it seemed quite natural.

'I can well believe it,' he said.

'The priest didn't,' snapped the farmer's wife. 'What did he say to you? Accused you of superstition, or something like that.'

'He said that angels weren't meant to be taken seriously,' said the farmer slowly. 'He said that they were symbols. Can you believe that? A priest saying that?'

'Astonishing,' said von Igelfeld. 'Angels are very important.'

'I'm glad to hear you say that,' said the farmer. 'The angels are really our only hope.'

They were silent for a moment, and von Igelfeld thought of angels. He would never see one, he was sure. Visions were reserved for the worthy, for people like this farmer who uncomplainingly spent his entire life on this little corner of land. Visions were a matter of desert.

'And then,' said the farmer. 'We had a major incident during the war – on that very hillside.'

Von Igelfeld looked at the hillside. It was quite unexceptional, with its innocent olive groves and its scattered oaks. What could have happened there? A terrible ambush perhaps?

'I was only eight then,' said the farmer. 'I was standing in the farmyard with my father and two of my uncles. All the trouble had passed us by, and so we were not worried when we saw the large American transport plane fly low overhead. We watched it, wondering where it was going, and then suddenly we saw a door in its side open and several parachutists jumped out. They floated down gently, coming to land on the hillside. Then the plane headed off over Montalcino and disappeared.

'We ran over to where the men had landed and greeted them. They smiled at us and said: "We're Americans and we've come to free you.'

'Well, we told them that we'd already been freed and that there was really nothing for them to do. So they looked a bit disappointed, but they came and had dinner with us. Then, after dinner, they went off to sleep in the barn, using their parachutes for bedding, and one of them went into the village. He never came back. He met a girl in the village and married her. The others were very cross and debated about going into the village to find him and shoot him, but they decided against it and instead went away on some bicycles they had requisitioned. My mother made shirts and underpants out of the parachutes. They lasted indefinitely, and I still occasionally wear them. That was it. That was the war. We've never forgotten it. It was so exciting.'

Von Igelfeld eventually bade a late and emotional farewell to his hosts and began the walk back to Montalcino. The pangs of hunger were a dim memory of the past; he would need to eat nothing that evening – that would show Signora Cossi! He entered the hotel, and hung his hat on one of the hat pegs. He was late, and dinner had already started. Then he remembered. Prinzel and Unterholzer had already arrived – he had totally forgotten about them – and there they were, at the table, tucking into the largest helpings of pasta which von Igelfeld had ever seen.

Von Igelfeld's heart sank. Look at them eat! It was enough to confirm Signora Cossi's views one hundred times over. And indeed it did, for as von Igelfeld stared in dismay at his companions, Signora Cossi swept out of the kitchen carrying two large plates, piled high with lamb cutlets.

'For your friends!' she said triumphantly, as she passed her speechless guest.

Prinzel and Unterholzer could not understand von Igelfeld's bad mood. Nor did they understand his expression of dismay when, after they had settled their bills, a smirking Signora Cossi handed von Igelfeld a small package.

'I saw you throw these away,' she said, giving him his laces. 'You must surely have done so by mistake.'

Her expression was one of utter, unassailable triumph, and von Igelfeld was to remember it well after he had forgotten his walks through that timeless landscape, that marvellous meal under the farmer's oak tree, and the vision, so generously shared, of angels.

PORTUGUESE IRREGULAR VERBS

THEY TOOK UP RESIDENCE IN REGENSBURG one by one – von Igelfeld first, then Unterholzer and finally Prinzel. Prinzel's new wife, Ophelia, had been reluctant to leave Wiesbaden, where she acted as secretary to her father in the Wiesbaden Project on Puccini. This project, which had been running for fourteen years, was set to run for at least a further decade, or more, and absorbed almost all the energies of both herself and her father. A move was quite out of the question.

At the time when Unterholzer moved to Regensburg, von Igelfeld was himself involved in his own difficulties over publication. Studia Litteraria Verlag, the publishers of his renowned and monumental work *Portuguese Irregular Verbs*, had written to him informing him that they had managed to sell only two hundred copies of the book. There was no doubt about the book's status: it was to be found in all the relevant libraries of Europe and North America, and was established as a classic in its field; but the problem was that the field was extremely small. Indeed, almost the entire field met every year at the annual conference and fitted comfortably into one small conference hall, usually with twenty or thirty seats left over.

The publishers pointed out that although two hundred copies had been sold, there still remained seven hundred and thirty-seven in a warehouse in Frankfurt. Over the previous two years, only six copies had been sold, and it occurred to them that at this rate they could expect to have to store the stock until well into the twenty-second century. Von Igelfeld personally saw nothing unacceptable about this, and was outraged when he read the proposal of Studia Litteraria's manager.

'We have received an offer from a firm of interior decorators,' he read. 'They decorate the apartments of wealthy people in a style which indicates good taste and education. They are keen to purchase our entire stock of *Portuguese Irregular Verbs*, which, as

you know, has a very fine binding. They will then, *at their own expense and at no cost to yourself*, change the embossed spine title to *Portuguese Irrigated Herbs* and use them as book furniture for the bookshelves they install in the houses of their customers. I am sure you will agree that this is an excellent idea, and I look forward to receiving your views on the proposition.'

It was no use, thought von Igelfeld, to attempt to use the arguments of scholarship and value when dealing with commercial men, such as the proprietors of Studia Litteraria undoubtedly were: they only understood the market. It would be far better, then, to ask them to wait for a while and see whether the sales of *Portuguese Irregular Verbs* picked up. From the commercial point of view, it would surely be more profitable to sell the book as a book, rather than as – what was the insulting expression they had used? – *furniture*.

Yet it was difficult to imagine sales picking up. There was no event, no anniversary, on the horizon to suggest that *Portuguese Irregular Verbs* might suddenly become more topical. Nor was von Igelfeld's own fame, though unquestioned in the field, likely to become markedly greater. No, any sudden increase in interest in the book would have to be the result of von Igelfeld's own efforts to persuade those who did not currently own a copy to buy one.

As an experiment, von Igelfeld wrote to his mother's cousin in Klagenfurt, Freiherr Willi-Maximilian Guntel, asking him whether the library in his country house contained a copy of the work. A prompt reply was received.

'*My dear Moritz-Maria,*' the letter ran. '*My failing health makes me something of a recluse these days, and it is therefore such a great pleasure to receive mail, especially from the family. How kind of you to offer to give me a copy of your book. I must admit that my library has little about Portugal in it. In fact, it contains nothing at all about Portugal. Your kind gift would therefore be most appreciated.*

Now, on another matter, do you remember cousin Armand, the thin one, who used to mutter so? Well, it really is the most extraordinary story . . . '

Von Igelfeld was, of course, trapped, and in due course the order department of Studia Litteraria was surprised to receive an order for a copy of *Portuguese Irregular Verbs*, with an accompanying cheque drawn on the account of the author, Professor Dr Moritz-Maria von Igelfeld. Clearly, caution would have to be shown in soliciting purchases, or it could become an expensive business.

Von Igelfeld thought again. What he should try to do is to find out by more indirect means who owned a copy and who did not. Unterholzer, for example: did he own a copy, or did he merely make free use of library copies?

'Unterholzer,' von Igelfeld said one day as the two philologists sat in the Café Schubert, drinking coffee. 'I've been thinking recently about updating *Portuguese Irregular Verbs*. What do you think?'

Unterholzer looked surprised. 'Does it need it?' he asked. 'Have the verbs changed recently? Becoming more regular?'

Von Igelfeld reacted crossly to what he thought was an unnecessarily flippant remark.

'Of course not,' he snapped. 'But scholarship always marches on. There have been several very important developments since the last edition.'

Unterholzer was apologetic. 'Of course, of course.'

Von Igelfeld glanced sideways at his friend. Now, perhaps, was the time to strike.

'But I wonder if people would want to buy a new edition . . . ' He paused, raising the coffee cup to his lips. 'Especially if they already have a copy.'

'They might,' said Unterholzer. 'Who knows?'

Von Igelfeld lowered his cup. 'Take somebody like you, for example. Would you buy a new edition?'

Von Igelfeld felt his heart pounding within him. He was astonished at his own sheer bravery in asking the question. Surely he had Unterholzer cornered now.

Unterholzer smiled. 'I should hope for a review copy from the *Zeitschrift*,' he said lightly.

Von Igelfeld was silent. Unterholzer had given nothing away. Could his remark have meant that he had received a review copy of the first edition? And if so, then where was the review? Von Igelfeld had not seen it. Or had Unterholzer really bought a copy of the first edition and was now hoping to be spared the cost of a second? That was conceivable, but how could one possibly tell?

As days passed, von Igelfeld's chagrin increased over the inconclusive nature of his discussion with Unterholzer. He realised that if he did not know whether or not even a close colleague like Unterholzer had a copy of *Portuguese Irregular Verbs*, then there would be little chance of encouraging sales. He could hardly tout the book on an indiscriminate basis; the only way would be by the subtle, individual approach.

It would have been simple, of course, if Unterholzer had kept his books in the Institute. Had that been the case, then all von Igelfeld would have had to do would be to cast an eye over his colleague's bookshelves on his next visit to his room. Unfortunately, Unterholzer was the only person in the Institute whose room was virtually devoid of books. He largely worked in the library, and his own collection, he had explained to everyone, was kept in his study at home.

Von Igelfeld pondered. He knew where Unterholzer lived, but he had never been in his flat. They had walked past it one day, and Unterholzer had pointed up at his windows and balcony, but no invitation had been extended to drop in for a cup of coffee. By contrast, Unterholzer had been invited to von Igelfeld's house five or six times; he had attended the party which von Igelfeld had thrown for Florianus and Ophelia Prinzel, and he had certainly been present at the stylish reception which von Igelfeld had held in honour of Professor Dr Dr (*h.c.*) (*mult.*) Reinhard Zimmermann. There was no doubt but that by any criteria of reciprocity of hospitality, Unterholzer should have invited von Igelfeld into his home.

[66]

Von Igelfeld decided to act. If Unterholzer was not going to invite him, then he must commit the solecism of arriving at the doorstep one day, uninvited. Unterholzer could hardly turn him away, particularly if it was raining, and in this way he would be able to inspect his bookshelves and settle once and for all the issue of whether he was the owner of *Portuguese Irregular Verbs*. All that was required was a rainy Saturday afternoon. Unterholzer would be in; von Igelfeld knew that he never went out, other than to go off on one of his solitary walks by the river; and not surprising, reflected von Igelfeld wryly – if he never issues any invitations then it's quite right that he should get none in return. In fact, the more he thought about it, the more unacceptable appeared Unterholzer's behaviour.

A suitably overcast Saturday afternoon arrived. Von Igelfeld made his way to the building in which Unterholzer lived. Standing outside, he looked up at the balcony which Unterholzer had pointed out and he noted with satisfaction that there was a light on inside. Good, he thought. Unterholzer was too mean to leave lights burning if he was not in.

Von Igelfeld peered at the plate above the bell and drew in his breath sharply. *Professor Dr Dr D-A. von Unterholzer*. What extra-ordinary, bare-faced cheek! It was little short of an outrage, on *three* counts, no less. Firstly, Unterholzer did not have two doctorates; there was no doubt about that. Secondly, what was all this nonsense about the hyphen between Detlev and Amadeus? Amadeus was his second name, as the whole world knew, not part of his first. And finally, and perhaps most seriously of all, there was the *von*. Von Igelfeld felt the anger surge up within him. If people got away with adding *vons* to their names whenever the mood took them, then that immeasurably reduced the significance of the real *vons*. So this was why Unterholzer had never invited him to his flat; it was simply because he knew that his pretensions would be exposed. But then, if nobody was ever invited, then who was there to be impressed by the bogus credentials? The postman? Or was it some bizarre, private fantasy on Unterholzer's part, designed to give him some inexplicable, solitary pleasure?

Von Igelfeld gave the bell an imperious, righteous push, in the way in which a policeman might ring a bell when he knew that a long-elusive quarry was hiding within. He heard the bell sounding and then, after a few moments, the door opened and Unterholzer stood before him.

'Good afternoon, Herr Unterholzer,' said von Igelfeld, throwing a glance in the direction of the name plate. 'I was walking past and the sky looked a bit threatening. I wondered if I might take shelter here for a while.'

Unterholzer frowned. 'The sky looked fine to me, when I last saw it.'

'It changes so quickly, though,' retorted von Igelfeld. 'The rain is definitely coming on.'

Unterholzer still looked unwilling to admit von Igelfeld.

'I'm also rather thirsty,' went on von Igelfeld. 'A glass of fruit juice would be most welcome.'

Unterholzer looked regretful. 'I'm afraid I have no fruit juice at the moment. There is, however, a small café round the corner.'

'Water would do quite well,' countered von Igelfeld. 'I take it that you haven't run out of that.'

It seemed to von Igelfeld that Unterholzer now had no alternative.

'Do come in,' the latter said. He suddenly became the genial host, as he ushered his guest into the hall and closed the front door behind him. 'Why don't we sit in my study?'

[68]

Von Igelfeld followed Unterholzer along a short corridor and into a large well-lit room. Two of the walls were covered with bookshelves, all of which were filled with books. There was a desk, on which sundry papers were scattered, a couch, and several arm chairs. It was a pleasant enough room, if somewhat spartan in its tone. It did not give the air of being well-used: none of the arm chairs looked as if they had ever been sat in, and on those shelves on which small ornaments were placed, these had been positioned strictly according to size.

Unterholzer gestured to the sofa while he himself sat in one of the arm chairs.

'I can't remember when you were last here,' he said to von Igelfeld, fixing him with a challenging stare.

Von Igelfeld pretended to search his memory. 'I can't remember either. It must have been a long time ago.'

He looked about the room, noting the cheap and unattractive framed views of the Rhine. It was not the sort of thing to which he would give wall space. It was almost kitsch in fact.

'I have a very good housekeeper,' said Unterholzer. 'Frau Kapicinska comes every morning. She keeps everything very clean.'

'That is very good,' said von Igelfeld. 'Is she Polish, by any chance?'

Unterholzer nodded. 'Yes. Polish.'

'Ah,' said von Igelfeld. 'I see.'

There was silence. Unterholzer looked up at the ceiling while von Igelfeld's gaze returned to the views of the Rhine. Really, they were terrible. They were coloured engravings – coloured well after the original had been printed. And there, facing these ill-depicted views of the Rhine, was a large framed photograph of a sausage dog. This was even worse. Could Unterholzer be one of those people who liked those unfortunate dogs? Von Igelfeld was aware of their popularity, but had always been irritated by what he considered to be the ridiculous appearance of the dachshund, with its absurd little legs and its long, sausage-like body. The von Igelfelds had always had large dogs, suitable for hunting on the plains of their now confiscated estates. They would never have owned a sausage dog. It was most irritating, really, to see these clichéd views of the Rhine and a sausage dog in such proximity.

'Do you have a dog, Herr Unterholzer?' asked von Igelfeld, looking about the room for signs of canine occupation.

Unterholzer smiled. 'Yes,' he said, proudly. 'I have a very fine dachshund. He is called Walter.'

Von Igelfeld raised an eyebrow. Walter? 'And does this dog live here, in this apartment?' he asked.

'He does,' said Unterholzer. 'He is sleeping now and we should not wake him up. But one day I will introduce you to him.'

'That would be very kind,' said von Igelfeld. He wanted to laugh, though, at the thought: Unterholzer saying to his ridiculous sausage dog, 'And this is Professor von Igelfeld' and von Igelfeld shaking the dog's proffered paw and saying, 'Good morning, Herr Unterholzer!' – because what else could he call the dog? He could hardly call him Walter on first meeting, and so it would have to be Herr Unterholzer. That, of course, would make it difficult to distinguish whether he was talking to Unterholzer or his dog, and could lead to confusion.

'Would you care for coffee?' Unterholzer asked suddenly. 'I could make some in the kitchen.'

Von Igelfeld accepted rapidly. He wanted to get Unterholzer out of the room for a few minutes so that he could check the book-shelves. It would not take long, but he could hardly do it while his host was present. And the moment that Unterholzer left, von Igelfeld was on his feet, his eye running rapidly over each shelf in turn. Not that one, nor that one; not there; no; *undsoweiter* until he had searched every shelf and reached the terrible, damning conclusion: Unterholzer did not own a copy of *Portuguese Irregular Verbs*.

When Unterholzer returned, he found von Igelfeld sitting in a different chair. He paid no attention to this; he had assumed that his guest would probably try to go through his papers in his absence. Well, there was nothing for him to find there; he was just wasting his time.

Von Igelfeld sipped at the coffee which Unterholzer had given him – not very good coffee, he noted. Was there anything to be said in Unterholzer's defence – anything at all? Could it be argued that he had suffered in some way, and that his suffering deserved sympathy? No. Unterholzer was not a refugee from the East or anything like that. Nor had he suffered at the hands of a cruel or bullying step-parent; von Igelfeld understood his father to be a perfectly reasonable retired bank manager. So there was no doubt but that Unterholzer was answerable for the various wrongs which had been so quickly and damningly chalked up against him.

As he thought this, von Igelfeld saw something else on the wall. It was a framed coat of arms, and underneath, in Gothic script, he made out: 'The arms of von Unterholzer'. Well, really! That was even worse than the views of the Rhine, which appeared to be in good taste by comparison.

Von Igelfeld bit his lip. Then he could remain silent no longer.

'I must say that I can't understand what you see in those views of the Rhine,' he said. 'Did some student give them to you?'

Unterholzer looked at the pictures and then looked at von Igelfeld.

'You mean you don't like them?' he asked.

'Yes,' said von Igelfeld icily. 'That's what I do mean. I think they're terribly, terribly vulgar.'

Unterholzer's jaw sagged open.

'Vulgar?' His voice was the voice of a broken man, but von Igelfeld pressed on.

'Kitsch, Herr Unterholzer,' he said. 'Kitsch. I gather that it's becoming fashionable again, but I didn't expect to find you, of all people, living in a . . . in a palace of kitsch!'

Unterholzer said nothing, as he looked about his study. Then, almost absent-mindedly, he offered von Igelfeld more coffee from his china coffee-pot with its curious chinoiserie pattern. Was that kitsch too, he wondered?

'Look out,' said von Igelfeld. 'You've splashed it on my shirt.'

With shaking hands, Unterholzer put down the coffee-pot.

'I'm terribly sorry,' he said. 'Do let me fetch a cloth.'

'No thank you,' said von Igelfeld coldly. 'Just you direct me to the bathroom and I'll attend to it myself.'

Von Igelfeld left Unterholzer in the study and walked angrily down the corridor to the bathroom. There he sponged off the two small coffee splashes and adjusted his tie. He closed the bathroom door behind him and started off down the corridor. There was a large bookshelf on his right, and from ancient habit he stooped to look at the contents. There, on the bottom shelf, standing out with their excellent bindings, stood not one, but two copies of *Portuguese Irregular Verbs*.

Von Igelfeld stood stock still. Then, cautiously, drew out the first copy and paged through it. It was well-used and had been annotated here and there in Unterholzer's characteristic script. *Precisely* read one comment; *confirmed by Zimmermann* said another.

He put the book back in its place and took out the second copy. This was in pristine condition, and had clearly been little used. He looked at the flyleaf to see if Unterholzer had stuck in his book plate, which he had not. Instead, in Unterholzer's writing again, there was the following inscription: *To my dear friend and colleague, in gratitude: the author, Moritz-Maria von Igelfeld.*

For a moment Von Igelfeld did not know what to think. Of course he had never given Unterholzer a copy; it had never occurred to him. But why should he then have decided to write his own inscription, as if a presentation had been made?

Von Igelfeld replaced the book on the shelf, straightened his tie again, and went back into the study. As he entered the room, he paused, looked at the views of the Rhine again, and stroked his chin pensively.

'You do know I was just joking a few minutes ago,' he said. 'Those really are very attractive pictures.'

Unterholzer looked up sharply, his eyes bright with pleasure. 'You don't think them kitsch?'

'Good heavens!' exclaimed von Igelfeld. 'Can't you take a joke, Herr Unterholzer? Kitsch! If those are kitsch, then I don't know what good taste is.'

Unterholzer beamed up at his guest.

'I have a cake in the kitchen,' he said eagerly. 'It's a cake cooked by Frau Kapicinska. Should I bring it through?'

Von Igelfeld nodded. 'That would be very nice,' he said warmly. 'A piece of cake is just what's required.'

While Unterholzer was out of the room, von Igelfeld put down his cup of coffee and moved over to examine the alleged crest of the von Unterholzers, and he was standing there when Unterholzer returned.

[73]

'It's a funny thing, Herr Unterholzer,' said von Igelfeld. 'But I've always thought that you might be *von* Unterholzer.'

Unterholzer laughed. 'It's not absolutely established,' he said. 'So I don't really use the *von* in public.'

'Of course not,' said von Igelfeld. 'But it's good to know you're entitled to it, isn't it?'

Unterholzer did not reply. He was busy cutting a large piece of cake. Frau Kapicinska had baked it five weeks ago and he hoped that it would still be fresh; he had no idea how long cakes could be expected to last.

Von Igelfeld's teeth sank into the cake. It was heavy and stale, but he would eat every crumb of it, he decided, and thank Unterholzer for it at the end. Indeed, he would ask for another piece.

HOLY MAN

AUDEN HAD CALLED SUCH PLACES 'weeds from Catholic Europe', and this is how Professor Dr Moritz-Maria von Igelfeld thought of them too; as usual, Auden's imagery struck him as so rich, so laden with associations, and when he received the letter from Goa, with its unfamiliar, faded stamp, the haunting metaphor crossed his mind again.

It was a thin, dejected-looking envelope, much tattered by its journey. Indeed, in one corner it appeared that some animal, possibly a dog, had bitten it, leaving small tooth holes. In another corner, the paper had split, revealing a single sheet of greying parchment within. Von Igelfeld turned it over and saw the address of the sender, typed erratically across the back flap: Professor J. G. K. L. Singh. The name made his heart sink: J. G. K. L. Singh of Chandighar, author of *Dravidian Verb Shifts*.

Impulsively, von Igelfeld tossed the letter into his wastepaper bin. It had clearly met with near disaster on its trip to Germany, von Igelfeld thought; had the dog swallowed it, then it would never have arrived at all. If he threw it away now, then he was merely fulfilling its manifest destiny.

Von Igelfeld turned away and picked up the next letter, a quiet, reassuring letter, with a solid, familiar, German stamp, and the name of the sender neatly typed in the right hand corner: Professor Dr Dr (*h.c.*) Florianus Prinzel. This was Prinzel's monthly letter, in which he would bring von Igelfeld up to date on developments in the Institute in Wiesbaden. At the end, penned in the slightly unsettling violet ink she habitually used, would be a small post-script from Ophelia Prinzel, with heart-warming domestic news of a trivial sort. This was exactly the sort of letter which von Igelfeld liked to receive, but even as he opened it and smoothed out the pages, his gaze turned guiltily to the poor, abandoned Indian letter, with its sad stamp and its flimsy paper.

Von Igelfeld wondered whether there was a moral obligation to read a letter. Surely the moral principles involved were the same as those which applied when somebody addressed a remark to one. One does not have to answer; but inevitably does. Yet, why should one have to answer: was there anything intrinsically wrong about ignoring somebody who said something to you if you hadn't asked them to say something in the first place? Von Igelfeld wondered what view Immanuel Kant had expressed on this subject. Would Kant have thrown Professor J. G. K. L. Singh's letter into his wastepaper basket? Von Igelfeld doubted it: the matter was clearly embraced by the Categorical Imperative. That settled that, but then the disturbing thought occurred: what would Jean-Paul Sartre have done if he had received a letter from J. G. K. L. Singh? Von Igelfeld suspected that Sartre might have had little compunction in doing as von Igelfeld had done, provided it made him feel authentic, but then, *and here was the crucial difference*, he would not have worried about it. Or would he?

Von Igelfeld laid aside the epistle from Prinzel and retrieved the letter from the bin. Slitting open the remains of the flap, he took out the grey sheet within and unfolded it.

'*Dear Professor von Igelfeld,*' he read. '*Greetings from Goa, and from your colleague, Janiwandillannah Krishnamurti Singh! I am down in this part of the world making arrangements for the All-India Union Congress of Philological Studies. We are meeting here in four months time and I wonder whether you will come to read a paper. All arrangements will be made, with despatch, by myself, and it will be very good to have some of you German fellows down in these parts again. The programme will be first class, and we shall have many excellent chin-wags. Please let me know . . .*'

Von Igelfeld sighed. Now that he had opened the letter, his questions about obligation seemed utterly answered. He would have to go: he was sure that Kant would agree.

The organising committee of the All-India Union Congress of Philology had made a booking for von Igelfeld in the old wing of the Hotel Lisboa. It was a large, rambling hotel, surrounded by shady verandahs. The gardens of the hotel were filled with bougainvilleas, frangipanis, palms, and there were winding paths that led to small, secluded summerhouses. Von Igelfeld was delighted. The air was scented with blossom; the sky was of an echoing emptiness; Europe and all its frenzy was far beyond any conceivable horizon. He sat in the wicker chair that occupied most of the minute balcony outside his room and looked out over the tops of the gently swaying palms. What a relief it was that Kantian ethics had pressed him into coming!

There had as yet been no sign of Professor J. G. K. L. Singh. One of the other committee members, Professor Rasi Henderson Paliwalar, had been detailed to meet von Igelfeld and to make sure that he was well settled in his hotel. Professor Rasi Henderson

Paliwalar appeared to have an intimate knowledge of the time-tables of the Indian State Railways and explained that Professor J. G. K. L. Singh was on his way to Goa, but was travelling by train and could not be expected to arrive for another thirty-six hours. This news had been conveyed to von Igelfeld apologetically, but it had in fact gladdened the recipient's heart. The Congress was not due to start for another three days, and of those three days at least one and a half could be enjoyed without any fear of encountering the author of *Dravidian Verb Shifts*.

Professor Rasi Henderson Paliwalar was much taken up with arrangements for the Congress and was relieved when von Igelfeld indicated that he could easily take care of himself until the opening session.

'I should like to look about Goa,' explained von Igelfeld. 'There is so much interesting architecture to see.'

'Indeed,' said Professor Rasi Henderson Paliwalar, sounding somewhat doubtful. 'Much of it is falling down, I'm afraid to say. In fact, all of India is falling down, all the time. Soon we shall have nothing but a fallen down country, all over. I am telling you. These people here appreciate none of the finer things of life.'

As he made these disparaging remarks, the professor pointed dismissively at the manager of hotel, who beamed encouragingly and made a small bow. Von Igelfeld looked up at the ceiling of the Hotel Lisboa. There was an elaborate cornice, but several parts were missing, having fallen down.

That evening, after he had taken a refreshing drink of mango juice on the main verandah, von Igelfeld ventured out onto the road outside the hotel. Within a few seconds he had been surrounded by several men in red tunics, who started to quarrel over him until a villainous-looking man with a moustache appeared to win the argument and led von Igelfeld over to his cycle-driven rickshaw.

'I shall show you this fine town,' he said to von Igelfeld as the philologist eased himself into the small, cracked leather seat. 'What do you wish to see? The prison? The library? The grave of the last Portuguese governor?'

Von Igelfeld chose the library, which seemed the least disturbing of the options, and soon they were bowling down the road, overtaking pedestrians and slower rickshaws, the sinister rickshaw man ringing his bell energetically at every possible hazard.

The library was, of course, closed, but this did not deter the rickshaw man. Beckoning for von Igelfeld to follow him, he took him through the library gardens and walked up to the back door. Glancing about him, the rickshaw man took out a small bunch of implements, and started to try each in the lock. Von Igelfeld watched in amazement as his guide picked the lock; he knew he should have protested, but, faced with such effrontery, words completely failed him. Then, when the door swung open, equally passively he followed the rickshaw driver into the cool interior of the Goa State Library.

The building smelled of damp and mildew; the characteristic odour of books which have been allowed to rot.

'Here we are,' said the rickshaw man. 'These books are very, very old, and contain a great deal of Portuguese knowledge. The Portuguese brought them and now they have gone away and left their books behind.'

Von Igelfeld moved over to a shelf to examine the contents. He picked up a large, leather-bound tome, and turned the pages. The paper was yellowed and rotting, but he could make out the title quite clearly: *A Jesuit in Portuguese Goa* by Father Goncavles

Persquites SJ. He laid it down and picked up the next one: *The Lives of the Portuguese Sailors* by Luis Valatar. This was in an even worse condition, and the binding fell away in his hands as he attempted to open the book.

'It is time to go now,' said the rickshaw man suddenly. 'I shall take you to the prison. There is more to see there.'

Von Igelfeld left the library sadly, imagining the desolation of the deserted, decaying books. Could Father Persquites have envisaged that Goa would come to this, and that his book would lie rotting and undisturbed until a chance hand should pick it up for a few moments? Could Valatar have envisaged his covers coming off at the hands of a casual visitor, who had effectively broken into the library to view its utter abandonment, in an era when the Portuguese navigators meant nothing any more?

The prison was just around the corner, an imposing fort of a building. Von Igelfeld wondered whether his guide would repeat his key-picking trick, but they rode past the front gate and turned round the corner. Here the rickshaw man dismounted and indicated to von Igelfeld that he should follow him to a small window in the outer wall of the prison.

'Look through there,' he said, gesturing to the window.

Von Igelfeld peered through the tiny opening. On the other side, through the thickness of the fortress wall, was the very heart of the prison, a vast hall topped by great barred skylights. Around the edges of the hall, men sat at tables and benches, quietly absorbed in their work of sewing pieces of cloth together.

'It is the tailoring workshop,' whispered the rickshaw man in von Igelfeld's ear. 'They are trying to make these no-good characters into good tailors, but they are wasting their time.'

Von Igelfeld found himself fascinated by the scene within. He watched intently as a stout man walked into the hall from the other end, accompanied by a warder. The prisoners momentarily stopped sewing and looked expectantly at their visitor.

'That is one of the governors of the prison,' whispered his guide. 'He is called Mr Majipondi and he is very rich because he sells all these suits these bad fellows make to merchants in the town. He is also a well-known murderer.'

Von Igelfeld stared as several of the prisoners approached the governor with their work. The governor nodded, and suits were given to the warder. Then he turned on his heels and left the room.

'Whom did he murder?' asked von Igelfeld.

The rickshaw man looked about him. 'He murdered his wife's brother's second wife's son,' he said in a surprised tone, as if that was something that von Igelfeld should have known. 'The Portuguese would have shot him. Now that they've gone, there's nobody to shoot people any more.' For a few moments he looked saddened, as if bereft. Then he added brightly: 'And now, would you like to see the municipal park?'

Von Igelfeld had had enough, and asked to be taken back to the Hotel Lisboa. The unorthodox approach of his guide was somewhat disturbing, and he could not imagine what strange angle he might present on the municipal park. It was safer, he thought, to return to the hotel and its restful gardens. He would have a mango juice, write a brief note to Prinzel and Unterholzer, and then retire early to bed. There would be time enough for the municipal park tomorrow.

The rickshaw driver was somewhat unwilling to bring the tour to an end, but eventually reluctantly agreed to return to the hotel.

'There are many interesting things happening in the municipal park,' he said sulkily. 'They should not be missed.'

'I'm sure that's true,' said von Igelfeld. 'But I have letters to write,' adding, for effect, 'Many letters.'

This appeared to impress the driver, who immediately nodded his compliance and began to cycle back with considerably more energy than before. Von Igelfeld sat back in the cracked red leather seat and reflected on what he had seen. He wondered whether anybody ever used the library, and who looked after it. He wondered about the prisoners in their hall: what crimes had they committed, what weight of guilt pressed upon their shoulders? And as for Mr Majipondi: how had his murder remained unpunished if everybody, including the rickshaw drivers of the town, knew about it? Then, what transpired in the municipal park – what dealings, what trysts, what tragedies? Was that, perhaps, where Mr Majipondi had murdered his wife's brother's second wife's son? He sighed. These were all such difficult questions, and they remained obstinately unresolved in von Igelfeld's mind for the rest of the journey and well into the hot, sleepless hours of the night.

Von Igelfeld awoke early the next morning and took his breakfast on the main verandah. The morning sky was white and brilliant; the trees were filled with chattering birds; and there were two fresh hibiscus flowers in a vase on his table. All of this effectively dispelled the anxieties of the night and put von Igelfeld in a good mood for the day's exploring. He was determined to resist any imprecations from rickshaw drivers and he would see what he wanted to see on foot. There were interesting old buildings all around the hotel, and these would suffice for the moment.

Von Igelfeld had noticed that there was a back entrance to the hotel gardens, used by the staff and for deliveries. He decided to leave by this route rather than by the front, as in this way he would

[82]

be able to avoid the rickshaw drivers. Adjusting his broad-brimmed white hat, he walked briskly out of the back gate into the undistinguished service road that lay outside.

Not far along this road he came upon a building which seemed to invite inspection. It was an extraordinary edifice, three storeys high, and built in that curious, heavy style which the Portuguese so admire. There were scrolls above each window, a top-heavy neo-classical portico, and a courtyard which appeared to be harbouring an uncontrolled jungle. Von Igelfeld stepped back and looked at the building. Many of the windows were broken, and there was a general air of desertion about the place. He was struck by the feeling of melancholy which seemed to hang about the building, as if the very stones felt the loss of pride.

Von Igelfeld ventured through the portico. There was a bench directly to the right, and a doorway boarded up. Another door was slightly ajar, but the room within seemed sunk in darkness. Von Igelfeld moved on and peered into the courtyard.

It was not quite as much a jungle as it had appeared from outside. Certainly there was a profusion of plants, but they had been cut back here and there, revealing odd pieces of broken statuary. There was a stone urn in the Roman style, a figure of a boy caught in mid-leap, both arms broken off, and a toppled stone vase which had been covered in creepers.

It was then that von Igelfeld saw the Holy Man. He was sitting on the ground, at the side of the courtyard, a small bag at his side and a staff propped up against the wall behind. He was watching von Igelfeld, and when the philologist gave a start of surprise, the Holy Man raised an arm in salute.

'Do not be afraid of me,' he called out. 'I am just sitting here.'

Von Igelfeld was at a loss as to what to do. He was an intruder, and felt almost guilty, but the friendly salute and the reassuring message had set him at his ease. He walked across to where the Holy Man was sitting and reached out to shake his hand.

'I am sorry to disturb you,' he said. 'I was merely admiring this beautiful old building.'

The Holy Man lifted his eyes and cast a glance around the courtyard.

'Is this beauty?' he said. He seemed to reflect for a moment, then: 'Yes, perhaps it is. There is beauty in everything, even an old building that is now just a home for rats and mice.'

'That is true,' said von Igelfeld. He thought of Germany, where there were no rats or mice any more. 'Sometimes it's difficult to find beauty in my own country. Even the very earth is sick there.'

The Holy Man shook his head sadly. 'Man is very destructive. That is why he can never be like God.'

'That is very true,' agreed von Igelfeld. 'If only God would show us.'

The Holy Man closed his eyes. 'He does show us, sir. Oh yes, he does show us. If only we are prepared to see.'

Von Igelfeld was silent. His suspicion that this was a Holy Man was being proved correct. But how should he address him? Should he call him guru, as he had read one might do in such circumstances? Was he a real guru, though, or was he of some lower, or even higher, rank in the gradations of holiness? The situation was distinctly difficult.

'You are quite right, O guru,' he ventured hesitantly. 'If only we would see.'

The Holy Man did not appear to object to being called guru, and this put von Igelfeld at his ease. He was beginning to feel excited about the encounter. This was the real East, and he felt as if he was being vouchsafed a glimpse of something denied to so many casual visitors who presumably saw nothing more than the library or the prison. He imagined, with pleasure, the envy which Prinzel and Unterholzer would feel when he came to tell them about his meeting with the Holy Man. It would be quite outside their experience, and they would really have nothing at all to say. They would have no alternative but to listen.

'May I sit down, guru?' he asked, pointing to the ground next to the Holy Man.

The Holy Man smiled, and patted the earth affectionately. 'This is the earth on which we may all sit down,' he said. 'Even the poorest, most miserable man may sit down on the earth. It is your friend. Yes, sit down; your friend is beckoning you.'

[85]

Von Igelfeld sat down, next to the small bag, and waited for the Holy Man to say something. For a few minutes there was silence, but not an awkward one. The Holy Man seemed to be concentrating on something in the middle distance, but after a while he turned and looked at his guest.

'I have a gift of seeing things in the lives of people,' he said suddenly. 'God has entrusted me with this power.'

'I see,' said von Igelfeld, adding, rather lamely, 'Most of us cannot see very far, I suppose.'

The Holy Man nodded. 'God has been very good to me. I have nothing in this life other than my stick here and this small bag. But I have great riches otherwise.'

Von Igelfeld made a mental note to remember this sentiment: it was exactly what a Holy Man should say. He would repeat it to Prinzel and Unterholzer, and they would, he hoped, feel humbled.

'Yes,' said the Holy Man. 'And I can see some things about your life. Would you like to hear them?'

Von Igelfeld felt his heart racing. Did he want to receive a message, whatever it might turn out to be, from this Holy Man? It could be something disturbing, of course, something quite discouraging; but when would another chance like this present itself? He would have to seize the opportunity.

'You are very kind,' he said. 'I should like to hear.'

The Holy Man closed his eyes. For a few moments he mumbled a chant of some sort, and then he spoke.

'There is one thing which is close, and one thing which is far,' he began. 'The close thing is a man who is coming here to meet you, in this place. I see water, and I see the water all about the man. He is from the North. That is all I see of that.' He paused. What on earth could that be, thought von Igelfeld? It made no sense at all.

[86]

'Then,' went on the Holy Man. 'There is the far thing. That is a plot. There are people plotting against you in a distant land. They are plotting something terrible. You must go back as soon as you can and deal with these wicked people and their plot. That is all I see in that department now.'

Von Igelfeld drew in his breath. This was a clear, unequivocal warning, of the sort that one could not ignore. Suddenly, Goa seemed threatening. Suddenly, the sense of optimism he had felt at the breakfast table departed and he felt only foreboding. How stupid to have asked the Holy Man for his visions. He had been as foolish as Faust: only torment lay that way.

The Holy Man now stood up and picked up his bag.

'I must continue with my search,' he said. 'There are many paths and it is late.'

Von Igelfeld rose to his feet, and fished in his pocket for a bank note. This he pressed into the Holy Man's hand.

'These are alms for you,' he said. 'They are to assist you on your way.'

The Holy Man did not look at the money, but quickly slipped it into his dhoti.

'You are a good, kind man,' he said to von Igelfeld. 'God will illumine your path. Most surely he will.'

Then, without further words, he strode away, leaving von Igelfeld alone in the courtyard with the broken statues and the sound of the rats creeping around in the undergrowth.

Back at the Hotel Lisboa, von Igelfeld was handed a large, cream-coloured envelope on which his name had been written in an ornate script. He thought it might be a letter from Professor Rasi Henderson Paliwalar, with some news of the next day's conference

[87]

proceedings, but it was not. It was, in fact, a letter from the President of the Portuguese Chamber of Commerce, inviting von Igelfeld to be the guest of honour, and speaker, at that evening's dinner of the Chamber. Von Igelfeld was astonished at the brevity of the notice, but assumed that this must be quite normal in Goa, where things appeared to be ordered differently from the way in which they were ordered in Germany, or anywhere else for that matter.

He spent the rest of the day reading and preparing a short talk for the meeting. He had decided that he would explain to the businessmen what philology was all about, and in particular draw their attention to recent developments in Portuguese philology. He was pleased with the talk, when he had finished it: it was not too simple, so he could not be accused of talking down to his audience; yet it assumed only the barest acquaintance with linguistic and philological terms. It would be ideal for such an audience.

The Portuguese Chamber of Commerce turned out to be one of the best buildings in Goa. The home of a seventeenth-century merchant, it had subsequently been converted into a banking hall, and when the bank failed, the merchants had taken it over as a club. Von Igelfeld was shown the Members' Room, a marvellous saloon with leather armchairs and mahogany writing tables, and then, when the members had assembled in the dining room, he was accompanied in by the President and seated at the top table.

The meal was delicious, and the conversation of the President most entertaining. He was an exporter of sultanas, as his father and grandfather had been before him. The world of sultanas, he informed von Igelfeld, was full of intrigue, and he revealed a few of the juicier details over the soup.

After the meal, while they were waiting for coffee, and before his speech, von Igelfeld ran his eye about the room. There were

[88]

about eighty guests, all men, all dressed in formal attire. Von Igelfeld looked at the physical types represented: the fat, prosperous merchants; the thin, nervous-looking accountants; the sly bankers; and then he stopped. There, halfway down the third table, was the prison governor, Mr Majipondi. Von Igelfeld was astonished. Surely it was inappropriate for a prison governor, even if he did have dealings with the town's merchants, to mix socially with those who corrupted him? And what about the murder? Did the members of the Chamber of Commerce know all about that? Was a blind eye turned here, as apparently it was everywhere else?

These perplexing questions in his mind, von Igelfeld heard the applause that followed his introduction and rose to his feet. As he spoke, he tried not to look at the table at which Mr Majipondi was sitting, but he felt the eyes of the prison governor upon him, weighing him up, imagining him in a prison suit, or peeling potatoes perhaps?

There was prolonged applause when von Igelfeld finished his talk. Several of the members, who were clearly moved by what had been said, banged their spoons on the table, until quietened by a gesture from the President. Then the President stood up, thanked von Igelfeld profusely, and invited questions from the members.

There was complete silence. The candle flames guttered in the breeze; a waiter, standing against a wall, coughed slightly. Then a member from the top table stood up and said:

'That was most interesting, Professor von Igelfeld. It is always enlightening to hear of the work of others, and you have told us all about this philology of yours. Now, tell me please: is that all you do?'

The silence returned. All the members looked expectantly at von Igelfeld, who, completely taken aback by the question, merely nodded his head.

'He says: yes,' said the President. 'Now, if there are no more questions, members may adjourn to the saloon.'

As he accompanied the President into the rather dowdy, high-ceilinged room which served as the saloon, von Igelfeld turned over in his mind the events of the past hour. He had been surprised that there were no further questions, but he thought that perhaps the merchants would wish to ask him these in the relative infor-mality of the saloon. He was sure that there must have been something which he had said which would have given rise to doubts that would need to be resolved. Had his point about pronouns been entirely understood?

The President steered von Igelfeld to a place near the large, discoloured fireplace and placed a glass of port in his hand. Then, beckoning to a small group of members standing nearby, he drew them over and introduced them one by one to von Igelfeld.

'And this,' said the President, 'is Mr Majipondi.'

Von Igelfeld, who had been bowing slightly to each member, looked up. He had taken the proffered hand in mid-bow and only now did he see the beaming face of the prison governor before him.

'I am most honoured to meet you,' said Mr Majipondi in a low, unctuous voice. 'Your talk was most informative. Indeed,' and here he turned to the President for confirmation, 'it was the most learned talk we have ever enjoyed in this Chamber.'

The President nodded his ready agreement.

Von Igelfeld tried to shrug off the compliment. He felt distinctly uneasy in the presence of Mr Majipondi, and his only wish was to get away. But the prison governor had moved closer and had reached out to touch the lapel of his suit with a heavy, ring-encrusted hand. He held the material between his fingers, as if assessing its quality, and then, reluctantly letting go, he returned his gaze to von Igelfeld's face.

'I am the governor of our little prison here,' he said. 'We are very concerned about rehabilitation. We are making silk purses out of sows' ears – that is my business!'

He laughed, challenging von Igelfeld to do the same. But von Igelfeld felt only repulsion, and he pointedly ignored the invitation.

'And what about murderers?' he suddenly found himself asking. 'Do you make them better too?'

Mr Majipondi gave a slight start (or did he? von Igelfeld asked himself). He was looking closely at von Igelfeld, his eyes tiny points of cunning in his fleshy face.

'We do not have many of those,' he said. 'In fact, if you listen to what people say, you'd think I'm the only one around.'

Von Igelfeld battled to conceal his utter astonishment. Was this Mr Majipondi confessing, or was he suggesting that the rumours were just that – rumours?

It was a situation quite beyond von Igelfeld's experience. Nobody in Germany would make such a remark – even an incorrigible murderer. Von Igelfeld believed that such people tended to look for excuses, and that they usually blamed their crimes on somebody else or on some abnormal mental state. Nobody accepted blame these days, and yet here in Goa, it was perhaps different, and a murderer could cheerfully confess to his crime with no sense of shame. Was it something to do with Eastern attitudes of acceptance? Could it be that if you were a murderer, then that was your lot in life, and it should be borne uncomplainingly? Was it something to do with karma? He looked at Mr Majipondi again, who returned his gaze with undisturbed equanimity.

'Do you mean that people accuse you, the prison governor, of being a murderer?' asked von Igelfeld at last, trying to sound astonished at the suggestion.

Mr Majipondi laughed. 'What people say about others is of no consequence,' he answered. 'The important thing is how you feel inside.'

It was the sort of answer which the Holy Man would have given, and it rather took von Igelfeld by surprise. As he pondered its significance, the President exchanged a glance with Mr Majipondi, who suddenly bowed and withdrew from the group. It was now the chance of Mr Verenyai Butterchayra to speak to von Igelfeld, and while this successful cutlery manufacturer engaged the visiting scholar in conversation, von Igelfeld was able from time to time to get a glimpse of Mr Majipondi again, holding forth elsewhere to the evident pleasure of his fellow guests.

The following day was the first day of the conference. Von Igelfeld listened courteously to every paper, skilfully concealing the intense boredom he felt as speaker after speaker made his trite or eccentric contribution to the debate. One paper stood out as excellent, though, and this, in von Igelfeld's mind, made the whole thing worthwhile. This was Professor Richimantry Gupta's report on Urdu subjunctives – a masterpiece which von Igelfeld resolved to attempt to secure for publication in the *Zeitschrift* – if it had not already been published.

Then, at four o'clock, the day's proceedings came to an end. Von Igelfeld slipped out of the hall as quickly as he could, hoping to be able to get some fresh air before the sun went down. He was not quick enough, though, to avoid the attention of the day's chairman, who seized his elbow and asked him his view of the day's proceedings.

Von Igelfeld was tactful. 'It's such a pity that Professor J. G. K. L. Singh has been delayed,' he said. 'How he would have enjoyed Professor Gupta's contribution.'

The chairman nodded his agreement. 'So sad,' he said. 'I do hope that he makes a quick recovery.'

'A recovery?' asked von Igelfeld. 'I was under the impression that he was merely delayed, not ill.'

The chairman shook his head. 'Oh my dear Professor von Igelfeld,' he said, his voice lowered. 'I thought that you knew. Professor J. G. K. L. Singh's train fell off a railway bridge and into a river. Our dear colleague was spared drowning, but was seriously inconvenienced by a crocodile.'

Von Igelfeld's dismay greatly impressed the chairman.

'I can see that you were fond of him,' he said. 'I am sorry to be the bearer of such ill tidings.'

Von Igelfeld nodded distractedly. The words of the Holy Man's prophecy were coming back to him quite clearly. *There is one thing which is close and one thing which is far. The close thing is a man who is coming here to meet you, in this place. I see water, and I see water all about the man. He is from the North.*

Could it be that at the very moment that the prophecy was being delivered, the girders of the bridge had given way and the ill-fated train had plunged down into the river? It was very sad for Professor J. G. K. L. Singh, of course, but what about the second part of the prophecy? The first part had been shown to be true, and this meant that somebody, somewhere, was plotting against von Igelfeld. Who could this be, and where? Were the plotters in Germany? If they were, then it would be night-time there and they would be asleep in their shameless beds. But as the day began, then the plotters would presumably resume their nefarious activities.

The thought chilled von Igelfeld, and a feeling of foreboding remained with him throughout the rest of the night and was still there in the morning.

The second day of the conference was worse than the first. Von Igelfeld delivered his own paper, and was immediately thereafter assaulted by a barrage of irrelevant and unhelpful questions. He was in a bad mood at lunch, and spoke to nobody, and in the afternoon his mind was too exercised with the prophecy and its implications to pay any attention to the proceedings. At the end of the afternoon, when the conference came to its end, he avoided the final reception and slipped off to the hotel to pack his bags. Then, settling his account and bidding farewell to the manager of the hotel, he drove out to the airport in an old, cream-coloured taxi and waited for the first available seat on a plane to Europe.

India, with all its colours, confusions and heartbreak, slipped below him in a smudge of brown. Von Igelfeld sat at his window seat and looked out over the silver wing of steel. It had been a mistake to visit Goa, he concluded. It might be that some achieved spiritual solace in India, but this had been denied him. His one encounter with a Holy Man – perhaps the only such encounter he would be vouchsafed in his life – had turned into a nightmare. There was no peace in that – only horrible, gnawing doubt. And at the back of his mind, too, was the image of Professor J. G .K. L. Singh in the muddy waters of the river and of the great jaws of the crocodile poised to close upon the helpless philologist. It was an awful, haunting image, and it brought home to von Igelfeld his great lack of charity in relation to Professor J. G. K. L. Singh. He would make up for it, he determined. He would send a letter to Chandighar with an invitation to the Institute in Regensburg, which could be taken up once Professor J. G. K. L. Singh got better. He would make it clear, though, that the invitation was only for one week; that was very important.

Dear, friendly, safe, comfortable Germany! Von Igelfeld could have kissed the ground on his arrival, but wasted no time in rushing home. His house was in order, and Frau Gunter, who housekept for him, assured him that nothing untoward had happened. For a moment von Igelfeld wondered whether she was a plotter, but he rapidly dismissed the unworthy thought from his mind.

He took a bath, dressed in an appropriate suit, and made his way hurriedly to the Institute. There he attended to his mail, none of which was in the slightest bit threatening, and then sat at his desk and looked out of the window. Perhaps there was nothing in it after all. Certainly the clear, rational light of Germany made it all seem less threatening: a Holy Man made no sense here.

Von Igelfeld decided to visit the Institute library to glance at the latest journals. He put away his letters, picked up his briefcase, and sauntered down the corridor to the library.

'Professor Dr von Igelfeld!' said the Librarian in hushed tones. 'We thought you would be away for another three days.'

'I have come back early,' said von Igelfeld. 'The conference was not very successful.'

He looked about him. Something was happening in the library. Two of the junior librarians were taking books out of the shelves in the entrance hall and placing them on a trolley.

'What's happening here?' asked von Igelfeld. Librarians were always busy rearranging and recataloguing; von Igelfeld thought that it was all that stood between them and complete boredom.

The Librarian looked at his assistants.

'Oh, a little reorganisation. A few books in here are being taken into the back room.'

Von Igelfeld said nothing for a moment. His eye had fallen on the trolley and on one book in particular placed there and destined for the obscurity of the back room. *Portuguese Irregular Verbs*!

Slowly he recovered his speech. 'Who suggested this reorganisation?' he asked, his voice steady in spite of the turbulent emotions within him.

The Librarian smiled. 'It wasn't my idea,' he said brightly. 'Professor Dr Unterholzer and one of our visiting professors suggested it. I was happy to comply.'

Von Igelfeld's breathing was regular, but deep. It was all clear now, oh so clear!

'And who was this visiting professor?' he asked icily.

'Professor Dr Dr Prinzel,' answered the Librarian. He looked curiously at von Igelfeld. 'If you disapprove, of course . . . '

Von Igelfeld stepped forward and retrieved the copy of *Portuguese Irregular Verbs* from the trolley. The Librarian gasped.

'Of course . . . ' he stuttered. 'I had no idea that that work was involved.' He snatched the tome from von Igelfeld and replaced it on the shelf. 'It will, of course, remain exactly where it was. I should never have agreed to its being put in the back room, had I known.'

Von Igelfeld walked home. He was tired now, as the journey had begun to catch up on him. But he knew that he would be able to sleep well, now that he had identified the terrible plot which had been made against him. He would take no action against Prinzel and Unterholzer, who would just see that *Portuguese Irregular Verbs* remained in its accustomed place of prominence. He would not even say anything to them about it – he would rise quite above the whole matter.

It was a course of action of which the Holy Man would undoubtedly have approved.

DENTAL PAIN

PROFESSOR DR MORITZ-MARIA VON IGELFELD
had excellent teeth. As a boy, he had been taken to the dentist
every year, but treatment had rarely been necessary and the dentist
had dismissed him.

'Only come if you have toothache,' he said to von Igelfeld.
'These teeth of yours will last you your life.'

Von Igelfeld followed this questionable advice, and never
thought thereafter of consulting a dentist. Then, shortly after his
return from the French Philological Forum in Lyons, he felt a
sudden, gnawing pain at the back of his lower jaw. He looked at his
mouth in a mirror, but saw nothing other than a gleaming row of
apparently healthy teeth. There were no mouth ulcers and there
was no swelling, but the pain made him feel as if a long, heated
needle was being driven into his bone.

He put up with it for a full morning, and then, after lunch,
when it seemed as if his mouth would explode in searing agony, he
walked to a dental studio which he had noticed round the corner
from the Institute. A receptionist met him and took his history with
compassion.

'You're obviously in great pain,' she said. 'Dr von Brautheim will take you next. She will finish with her patient in a few minutes.'

Von Igelfeld sat down in the reception room and picked up the first magazine he saw on the table before him. He paged through it, noticing the pictures of food and clothes. How strange, he thought – what sort of *Zeitschrift* is this? Do people really read about these matters? He turned a page and began to read something called the *Timely Help* column. Readers wrote in and asked advice over their problems. Von Igelfeld's eyes opened wide. Did people discuss such things in open print? How could anybody talk about things like that? He read a letter from a woman in Hamburg which quite took his breath away. Why did she marry him in the first place, if she knew that was what he was like? Such men should be in prison, thought von Igelfeld, although that was not what the readers' adviser suggested. She said that the woman should try to talk to her husband and persuade him to change his ways. Well! thought von Igelfeld. If I wrote that column I would give very different advice. In fact, I should pass such letters over to the police without delay.

The door of the surgery opened and a miserable-looking man walked out. He put on his coat, massaged his jaw, and nodded to the receptionist. Then von Igelfeld was invited in, and found himself sitting in the dental chair of Dr Lisbetta von Brautheim. It was a new experience for him; the only dentist he had ever consulted had been a man. But there was nothing wrong with a woman dentist, he thought; in fact, she was likely to be much more sympathetic and gentle than a man.

Dr von Brautheim was a petite woman in her mid-thirties. She had a gentle, attractive face, and von Igelfeld found it very easy to look at her as she peered into his mouth. Her hands were careful as she prodded about in the angry area of his mouth, and even when her pick touched the very source of the pain, von Igelfeld found that he could bear the agony.

'An impacted supernumerary,' said Dr von Brautheim. 'I'm afraid the only thing I can do is remove it. That should give you the relief you need.'

Von Igelfeld nodded his agreement. He was utterly won over by Dr von Brautheim and would have consented to any suggestion she made. He opened his mouth again, felt the prick of the anaesthetic needle, and then a marvellous feeling of relief flooded over him. Dr von Brautheim worked quickly and efficiently, and within minutes the offending tooth was laid on a tray and the gap had been plugged with dressing.

'That is all, Professor Dr von Igelfeld,' she said quietly, as her instruments were whisked away into the steriliser. 'You should come back and see me the day after tomorrow and we shall see how things have settled down.'

Von Igelfeld arose from the couch and smiled at his saviour.

'The pain has gone,' he said. 'I thought it would kill me, but now it has gone.'

'Those teeth can be quite nasty when they impact,' said Dr von Brautheim. 'But otherwise your mouth looks very healthy.'

Von Igelfeld beamed with pleasure. To receive such a compliment from the attractive Dr von Brautheim gave him a considerable thrill, and as he walked down the stairs he reflected on his good fortune in being able to see her again so soon. He would bring her a present to thank her for her help – a bunch of flowers perhaps. Was she married, he wondered? What a marvellous wife she would make for somebody.

There was no more pain that night, nor the next morning. Von

Igelfeld dutifully swallowed the pills which Dr von Brautheim had given him and at the Institute that day he regaled everybody with the story of the remarkable cure which had been effected. The others then told their own dental stories: the Librarian related how his elderly aunt had lost several teeth some years before but was now, happily, fully recovered; the Deputy Librarian had an entire row of fillings, following upon a childhood indulged with sweets; and the Administrative Director revealed that he had in fact no teeth at all but found his false teeth very comfortable indeed.

That afternoon, von Igelfeld sat in his room, the proofs of the next issue of the *Zeitschrift* on his desk before him. He was wrestling with a particularly difficult paper, and was finding it almost impossible to edit in the way which he felt it needed to be edited. 'Spanish loan words,' wrote the author, 'appear to be profuse in Brazilian dialects, particularly those used by river-men. But are they really loan words, or are they Brazilian misunderstandings of Portuguese originals . . . '

Von Igelfeld looked up from the paper and stared out of his window. No matter how hard he tried to concentrate, his mind was distracted. What were these river-men like? He tried to picture them; tough-looking men, no doubt, with slouch hats; characters from a Conrad story, perhaps. But the image faded and his thoughts returned to the memory of his trip to the dental studio and of the sweet face of Dr von Brautheim above him. What did she think of her patients, and of their suffering? He imagined her as a ministering angel, gently bringing relief to those in pain. Von Igelfeld recalled the touch of her hands and the delicious smell of the soap, a reassuring, almost-nursery smell. To be looked after by such a being must be paradise indeed. Just imagine it!

He got up from his desk and walked about his room. Why was

it that he kept thinking of her, when he should have been thinking of the *Zeitschrift*? This had only happened to him once or twice before, and he distrusted the feeling. It had happened once when he was nineteen, and he had met, for a mere afternoon, the daughter of his Uncle Ludwig's neighbour. She had been at the conservatory in Berlin and had played her viola for him. He had seen her once or twice after that and then she had gone to America and never come back. He imagined a crude fate for her in the United States – living in a characterless apartment block with urban ugliness all about and a husband who growled and talked through his nose.

Von Igelfeld left his room and walked down the corridor to Unterholzer's small study. Unterholzer was in, leafing through his share of the *Zeitschrift* proofs, shaking his head disapprovingly.

'These printers,' he said to von Igelfeld. 'They must be illiterate. Here's a page with the diacritical marks all in the wrong place. They'll have to reset the whole thing.'

Von Igelfeld nodded absent-mindedly.

'I went to the dentist yesterday,' he announced. 'I was in great pain.'

Unterholzer looked up, concerned.

'I'm sorry to hear that. Did he fix everything up?'

'She,' said von Igelfeld, smiling. 'It was a lady dentist. And she made everything much better.'

'Oh,' said Unterholzer, his eyes returning to the proofs. 'I'm happy to hear that you're no longer in pain.'

Von Igelfeld crossed Unterholzer's room and looked disapprovingly out of the window: in contrast to the view from his own room, Unterholzer had a very unedifying view of the Institute car park. Perhaps it was good enough for him; poor Unterholzer.

'Yes,' he said. 'She was a very charming dentist indeed.

Very charming. In fact, I certainly would not mind pursuing her acquaintance.'

'Is that so?' said Unterholzer, still looking at the proofs. 'Perhaps I should go and have my teeth checked. Where is her studio?'

'Just round the corner,' said von Igelfeld. 'And it's a good idea to go to the dentist regularly, you know. When did you last go?'

'About a year or two ago,' said Unterholzer vaguely.

Von Igelfeld tut-tutted. 'That's not frequently enough,' he said. 'Dr von Brautheim recommends a visit once every six months.'

'Don't worry,' said Unterholzer. 'I'll make an appointment soon.'

Von Igelfeld gave up. He had hoped to be able to tell Unterholzer a little bit more about Dr von Brautheim, but he was clearly not going to be at all receptive. That was the trouble with Unterholzer, he thought – he was too literal. He had very little imagination.

On the appointed day, von Igelfeld dressed with care for his visit to the dental studio. He put on the bright red tie he had bought in Rome, and he took especial care in choosing his shirt. Then, with at least half an hour in hand, he made his way to the dental studio, carrying with him the present he had decided to give Dr von Brautheim. It was not a present which he usually gave to people, as it was not at all inexpensive. But Dr von Brautheim was different, and he had carefully wrapped it in soft purple paper he had acquired from a gift shop near his house.

He intended to do more than give her a present, though. He had decided that he would enquire discreetly of the receptionist whether her employer was single, and if that was the case – Oh bliss! – then he would ask her to join him for lunch some weekend. He would set up a lunch party – perhaps Zimmermann might come – and that would be a good setting in which to get to know her better.

The receptionist did not appear surprised by the question.

'Dr von Brautheim is unmarried,' she said. 'She lives with her elderly parents. Her father was Professor of Dentistry in Cologne.'

Von Igelfeld was delighted with this information. What a perfect background for such a person! Dentistry might not be the most prestigious career, but it was an honourable calling and people were wrong to look down upon it. And undoubtedly the von Brautheim family had once done something better, as the name suggested distinction of some sort.

He was admitted into the studio and, blushing slightly, took his place in the chair.

Dr von Brautheim took no more than a few minutes to attend to his mouth.

'It's healing nicely,' she said. 'And I see no complications. You may rinse your mouth out now.'

Disappointed at the brevity of the treatment, von Igelfeld became flustered. He had intended to raise the subject of the lunch party at this stage, but there was something about the situation which suggested that it would be inappropriate. There was still the present, though, and as he stood at the doorway he thrust it into her hands.

'This is a small token of my appreciation,' he said formally. 'You've been so kind.'

The dentist smiled, a warm, melting smile that made von Igelfeld feel weak at the knees.

'How kind of you Professor Dr von Igelfeld,' she said. 'How unnecessary, but how kind. May I open it now?'

'Of course,' said von Igelfeld. 'I should be delighted.'

Dr von Brautheim unwrapped the soft purple paper and there it was, in her hands, *Portuguese Irregular Verbs*!

'How kind!' she repeated. 'Such a large book too!'

Over the next week, von Igelfeld thought of little else. He had decided that he would leave it about ten days before he sent the note inviting her to the lunch, which would be held a month after that. This would mean that it would be unlikely that she would have another commitment and would therefore accept. In due course the letter was written, and a prompt reply received. Yes, she would be delighted to attend his lunch party on the stated date.

Meanwhile, Unterholzer announced that he had himself consulted Dr von Brautheim, who had suggested two fillings and a new crown. He was delighted with her treatment, and told von Igelfeld that for the first time in his life he found himself looking forward to being in the dentist's chair. Von Igelfeld found this rather presumptuous, but said nothing.

A few days before the lunch party was due to take place, von
Igelfeld decided that he could properly call on Dr von Brautheim
again to give her directions as to how to reach his house. It was not
strictly speaking necessary, as she would undoubtedly have a map of
the town, but it would give him an opportunity to see her again.

He made his way up to the dental studio, his heart hammering
with excitement. The receptionist greeted him warmly and asked
him whether he was experiencing further trouble with his teeth.
Von Igelfeld explained his mission, and was disappointed when the
receptionist told him that it was Dr von Brautheim's afternoon off
and that she would not be in until tomorrow.

'You may leave her a note, though,' she said.

Von Igelfeld glanced towards the studio, the door of which was
open. There was the drill apparatus, the couch, the chest of
instruments, and there, on the floor beside the chair was *Portuguese
Irregular Verbs*. For a moment he said nothing. Then a wave of
emotion flooded through him. She was reading his book in
between patients! What a marvellous, wonderful thing!

'That book,' he said to the receptionist. 'Is Dr von Brautheim
reading it at present?'

The receptionist glanced in the direction of the studio and
smiled. 'That? Oh no. You know that Dr von Brautheim isn't very
tall, and she's found that standing on that book brings her up to
just the right height for when the chair's reclined.'

Von Igelfeld left a brief note, confirming the time and place of
the lunch. Then he went out into the street, his mind in turmoil.
No, he should not take offence, he told himself. It was quite
touching really. It was unfair to expect everybody to be interested
in philology, and at least she had found a use for the book. Perhaps
she even used it because it reminded her of him! Yes, that was it. If

he looked at it that way, then the ignominious fate of *Portuguese Irregular Verbs* was nothing to worry over.

He made his way into the Institute and settled down to the work that had piled up over the last few weeks of distraction. There was a great deal to do, and when six o'clock came he had made little impression on it. Most of the staff of the Institute had left, and von Igelfeld was surprised when Unterholzer knocked at his door.

'What's keeping you in, Unterholzer?' von Igelfeld asked.

Unterholzer stood in the doorway, beaming with pleasure.

'I'm in because I've been out,' he said. 'I took the afternoon off and now I've come in to do what I wanted to do during the afternoon.'

'Oh yes,' said von Igelfeld, with a distinct lack of interest. 'What did you do?'

Unterholzer stepped forward into the room.

'I went out . . . ' he began, halting in his excitement. 'I went out with my new fiancée. We went to buy a ring.'

Von Igelfeld dropped his pen in amazement.

'Your new fiancée!' he exclaimed. 'Unterholzer, what dramatic news! Who is she?'

'My dentist!' crowed Unterholzer. 'The delightful Dr von Brautheim. I have been seeing her regularly and we have fallen in love with one another. At lunch time she agreed to become my wife. I shall be calling on her father tomorrow. Do you know that he had the Chair of Dentistry in Cologne?'

Von Igelfeld stayed in the Institute until half past eleven, alone with his papers. Then he walked home, following his usual route, reflecting on the sadnesses of life – visions unrealised, love unfulfilled, dental pain.

DEATH IN VENICE

THE WEDDING OF Professor Dr Detlev Amadeus Unterholzer and Dr Lisbetta von Brautheim was a particularly trying occasion for the author of *Portuguese Irregular Verbs*. Von Igelfeld tried to rise above the feelings of resentment he experienced on finding that Unterholzer, of all people, had succeeded in securing the affections of the woman he had been planning to marry, but it was difficult. If only he had not waited; if only he had invited her to lunch immediately, rather than a full five weeks later, then matters would have turned out differently. And, of course, if he had not been so foolish as to recommend that Unterholzer have his teeth seen to, then the couple would never have met and it would have been him, rather than Unterholzer, standing beside Lisbetta at the altar.

Such thoughts, of course, led nowhere. Von Igelfeld put on as brave a face as he could, and tried to show pleasure in the evident happiness of the bride and groom. At the wedding itself, a large occasion attended by over two hundred people, he sat next to Florianus and Ophelia Prinzel, and this helped to take his mind off the thought of what might have been. Ophelia Prinzel found weddings extremely moving occasions and wept voluminously, with Prinzel and von Igelfeld taking it in turns to comfort her.

Later, though, von Igelfeld confessed to Ophelia what had happened, and she was aghast at the story.

'What awful, awful bad luck,' she said sympathetically. 'You would have made a much better husband for her, Moritz-Maria. Unterholzer's all very well, but . . . '

Von Igelfeld nodded. 'I know,' he said. 'But it's too late now, and I suppose we must wish them every happiness.'

Ophelia Prinzel agreed that this was the charitable thing to do, but she was secretly thinking of what it would be like to share a bed with Unterholzer and the notion did not appeal. In fact, she closed her eyes and shuddered.

'However,' she said, 'there's no point in thinking of what might have been. The important thing is: how do you feel?'

For a moment von Igelfeld said nothing, then he turned to her and said, 'Terrible! I feel all washed up and finished. I feel as if there's no point to life any more, even to my work. What's the use? Where does it all lead?'

Ophelia laid a comforting hand on his shoulder.

'You need to get away,' she said. 'You must come with us to Venice, mustn't he, Florianus?'

Prinzel quickly agreed with his wife. 'We're going to go in two months time. We shall spend a month there in September, when the worst of the crowds have gone. You'd be very welcome, you know.'

Von Igelfeld thought for a moment. He usually went to Switzerland in the late summer, but it was a good three years since he had been to Venice and perhaps it was just what he needed. In Switzerland he always walked and climbed – it was really no holiday – whereas in Venice he could take things very easily, read, and enjoy good Italian meals. Yes, it was an excellent idea altogether.

The Prinzels travelled down to Venice first, motoring in a leisurely way through the hills of Austria. Von Igelfeld followed by train, and when his carriage eventually drew into Venice station, there was Prinzel to meet him. They boarded a *vaporetto* and were soon heading out across the lagoon, through that waterscape of legend, past the proud liners at anchor, past the tether posts, past the cypress-crowned islands. Von Igelfeld watched as the city retreated and the Lido drew near, and then they were ashore, and a liveried porter of the Grand Hôtel des Bains was struggling with the von Igelfeld cabin trunks, the very same trunks which his grandfather had himself brought to the beguiling city.

Established in his room overlooking the hotel gardens and the beach, von Igelfeld changed out of his suit and donned a white linen jacket and lightweight trousers. Then, with his Panama hat in hand, he made his way down to the main terrace where Prinzel and Ophelia were waiting for him. They sat and drank lemon tea, chatting for over an hour, and then von Igelfeld returned to his room for a siesta. He was already beginning to feel relaxed, and he knew that Ophelia's advice had been sound. How pointless in such surroundings to worry about lost chances and the petty irritations of life! Here all that mattered was art and beauty.

He slept deeply, awaking shortly after six o'clock. Drawing his curtains, he noticed that the sun was setting over the city, a great red ball sinking behind the distant domes, setting fire to the pale blue water. He stood for a few minutes, quite entranced, and then he left his room and went down to the terrace again. They had all agreed to meet for dinner at eight, and until then, von Igelfeld sat on the terrace, reading the copy of *I Promessi Sposi* which he had extracted from one of his cabin trunks. It was a perfect evening, and the hours before dinner went rather too quickly for von Igelfeld. He could have sat there forever, he thought, looking at his fellow guests and the bobbing lights upon the sea.

They dined in the main dining room. Ophelia chose all the courses, and every one of them was approved of by von Igelfeld. The conversation was light and entertaining: neither Unterholzer nor Dr von Brautheim was mentioned once, although the occasional painful memory momentarily crossed von Igelfeld's mind. After dinner, they returned to the terrace to drink small cups of strong, scalding coffee.

'This is perfect,' said von Igelfeld. 'I could stay here indefinitely, I'm sure.'

Prinzel laughed. 'You think you could,' he said. 'But remember, we're only visitors. The reality of Venice might be rather different when one's exposed to it all the time. This city has other moods, remember.'

'Oh?' said von Igelfeld. 'What do you mean by that?'

Prinzel paused before answering. 'It's corrupt. Some say that it's dying. Can't you smell it? The decay?'

Von Igelfeld thought about this for some time, and later on, in the small hours of the morning, he was troubled by a dreadful nightmare. He was alone in a small Venetian street, a street that appeared to lead nowhere. At every corner there were mocking figures wearing elaborate Venetian masks, laughing at him, ridiculing him. He sat up in bed and shivered. He had left the window slightly open, and a breeze was moving the curtains. He turned on a light, looked at his watch, and took a long draught of mineral water. What was wrong? Why had Prinzel said that Venice was dying? What had he meant?

The next morning, with the sun streaming in through his

window, von Igelfeld was able to put the terrors of the night well behind him. He showered, once again donned his light linen jacket, and went downstairs for breakfast. They had agreed to pursue their own activities and interests during the day and to meet each evening for dinner – a good arrangement, von Igelfeld thought, as they didn't want to be too much on top of one another.

Sitting at the starched white cloth of his table, von Igelfeld smiled as he addressed his breakfast. He looked at the twenty or so other guests who were making an early start to the day. There was a young couple, absorbed in each other, with eyes for nobody else; there was an elderly woman with purple-rinsed hair, American, thought von Igelfeld, and lonely; there was a clergyman of some sort, probably English, von Igelfeld decided; and then there was a large family, of mother, governess and four children. Von Igelfeld watched the family. They were elegantly and expensively dressed, three girls and a boy. The girls wore light blue dresses and ribbons in their hair – almost a family uniform – and the boy, who was about fifteen or sixteen, wore a sailor suit.

Von Igelfeld's eye passed to the mother. What a beautiful woman she was, he thought, and she was so clearly used to admiration and respect, as she sat with an air of almost palpable authority, speaking to each of her children in turn, occasionally saying something to the governess. 'Where is father?' he wondered. Was he still working in some distant city, supporting this expensive family in luxury, or had something terrible happened to him? Certainly the mother did not look like a widow; she was vivacious and carefree, whereas widows, in von Igelfeld's experience, *pace* Franz Lehar, never were.

Von Igelfeld buttered a further roll and allowed honey to drip all over it. Then he took another sip of coffee and glanced over at the family's table again. As he did so, the boy turned his head and looked directly at him. Von Igelfeld dropped his gaze, but he felt that the boy was still staring at him. He concentrated on his roll. Had the honey been evenly spread, or was it too concentrated at the one end? He looked up again and the flaxen-haired boy was still staring in his direction with wide blue, inquisitive eyes. Von Igelfeld fingered at the knot in his tie and turned away. He was accustomed to being stared at, being so tall, but it always made him feel uneasy. The mother should teach him not to stare, he thought; but parents appeared to teach their children nothing these days.

After he had finished his roll, von Igelfeld poured himself another large cup of strong, milky coffee, and drained it with pleasure. The family had arisen from the table now, and was trooping out of the dining room. The boy was the last to go, and as he left he turned and glanced at von Igelfeld, tossing his hair back as he did so. Von Igelfeld frowned, and looked down at his tie. Was there something odd in his dress that made the boy look at him? Did his shoes match? Of course they did.

He walked out onto the terrace and felt the morning sun on his face. It was going to be a marvellous day, although it could well become a little warm at noon. He would go to the *Accademia* this morning, he told himself, and then afterwards he would seek out the peace of one of the quieter churches. He had always liked the church of San Giovanni Cristostomo, and perhaps he would spend an hour or so there looking at Bellini's *St Jerome with St Christopher and St Augustine*. That would keep him busy until lunchtime, which he would spend in a small restaurant which he always visited when he was in Venice and where he was known to the proprietor. After lunch he could return to the hotel, sleep, and then meet the Prinzels for dinner. It would be a most satisfactory day.

The *Accademia* was surprisingly quiet. Von Igelfeld wandered from room to room, feasting his eyes on the great, brooding paintings. By mid-morning he was in Room Seven, standing before Lotto's *Portrait of a Young Man in his Study*. Von Igelfeld gazed at the great canvas, his eye moving over the objects which made up the young man's world – the mandolin, silent, but a reminder of the carefree pleasure of youth (he thought of Heidelberg, and of the easy fellowship of student years, never, never recaptured); the hunting horn (*Als ich ein Junge war*, muttered von Igelfeld); and there, on the ground, the painter had painted the fallen rose petals – his final statement on the transience of life. Von Igelfeld walked away, throwing a glance over his shoulder at the picture. Suddenly, for no reason at all, he thought of the boy in the hotel. *He* could play the mandolin, no doubt, and blow the hunting horn too, for that matter. But would he come back, thirty, forty years from now and look at this picture, just as von Igelfeld was now doing? Perhaps he would.

In San Giovanni Cristotomo von Igelfeld was virtually by himself. He sat on a chair near a confessional, gazing up at the ceiling, letting the stress of the city drain out of his limbs. The sun filtered in through a high window, a dusty yellow shaft, the colour of butter. Von Igelfeld closed his eyes and thought: I'm in a house of God, but who is he? Where is he, this person he had always addressed as God but who had never spoken back to him, ever. He was not sure about the existence of God, but he had always been convinced that if he did exist, he would be the God of Mediterranean Christianity, not the cold, hard God of the Northern churches. But that, perhaps, was to draw too much comfort; he might even turn out to be the God of the quantum physicists, a final point implosion, or perhaps just a single particle, a tiny event. That would be terribly disappointing – if God were to prove to be an electron.

He opened his eyes. A group had entered the church and was making its way across the nave. It was a family, and von Igelfeld noticed with a sudden shock that it was the family from the hotel. He watched cautiously as the mother pointed towards the altar. One of the girls asked a question and the mother handed her a guidebook. Then the boy in the sailor suit stepped forward and tapped at his mother's elbow. She listened to him for a moment, and then laughed. Sulking, he moved away, walking towards von Igelfeld. Now he was in the shaft of sunlight, and for a moment he appeared to be an angel, from Giorgione's studio, perhaps, clothed in the softness of the light, glowing with gold.

Suddenly the boy looked in von Igelfeld's direction. When he saw the professor, he gave a slight start, but then smiled, and again, as at the breakfast table, he stared. Von Igelfeld did not know what to do. Should he acknowledge the youth, or should he ignore him? He could hardly pretend not to have seen him, and yet he had no desire to do anything which would concede to the boy that he had any right to intrude on his privacy as he was so clearly doing. What did this boy want of him after all? The whole situation was peculiar; familiar in a curious, inexplicable way; redolent of something he had read somewhere; but where?

The mother came to von Igelfeld's rescue.

'Tadseuz!' she called. 'Viens ici! Nous allons voir quelque chose de grand interêt . . . '

Tadseuz! thought von Igelfeld. So they are Polish. How very interesting! Perhaps Polish boys are particularly given to staring at people. The Poles were definitely very strange about certain things, and this might be one of them. He rose to his feet and slipped out of the church before the boy could bother him any further. His restaurant was just round the corner, and there, at least he would be safe from the unwelcome attentions of Polish boys.

'*Caro* Dottor von Igelfeld!' exclaimed the proprietor of the restaurant. 'Here you are again! We turn our back for two or three years, and, *Caspita*, there you are again!'

He led von Igelfeld to a table in a quiet corner and summoned a waiter. Von Igelfeld felt a warm rush of satisfaction; he knew that to the proprietor he was no more than a client whose name had happened to lodge in the mind, but he felt as if he was amongst friends.

A bottle of chilled wine from the hills was produced and the proprietor filled a glass for himself as well as for von Igelfeld.

'We are so glad to see you,' he said, raising his glass in toast. 'There are fewer people coming these days. This summer there were virtually no Germans in Italy. It was terrible!'

'No Germans!' Von Igelfeld was astonished at the hyperbole, but the proprietor seemed serious.

'They are keeping away from Venice for some reason,' he went on. 'They say it is something to do with the sea.'

'Is there anything wrong with the sea?' von Igelfeld asked, thinking of the beach at the Grand Hôtel des Bains. There had been people on it, hadn't there?

The proprietor shook his head vigorously. 'No! No! The sea is still there. The sea is fine. No, there is no reason for the Germans not to come.'

Von Igelfeld was puzzled and would have continued the discussion, but the proprietor clearly wanted to change the subject and he drew von Igelfeld's attentions to certain items on the menu.

'These are very good,' he said enthusiastically, drawing attention to the scallops. '*Scallopini alla Marie Curie*. I shall supervise their cooking personally. You will not be disappointed.'

After lunch, which lasted for over two hours, von Igelfeld walked back slowly towards the landing stage where he could board a *vaporetto* for the Lido. The back streets were quiet, and his footsteps rang out against the walls of the houses. Somewhere above him, in one of the windows, a woman was singing – a snatch of song, an aria that he had heard before but could not quite place. He stopped and listened. The singing continued for a few minutes and then it faded. Now a cat called somewhere in a doorway and there was the sound of a lock being turned.

Von Igelfeld went on. At the end of the street, the pavement took a turn and ran for a few yards to a small bridge across the canal. As he reached this point, von Igelfeld noticed two men clad in white crouching down beside the water. The men were unaware of his presence and he watched them as they dipped a container of some sort into the canal. Then they took it up and decanted a small quantity of water into a bottle. One of the men shook his head, while the other wrote something in a notebook. Then they stood up, and came face to face with von Igelfeld.

'*Scusi*,' said one of the men, and the two then bustled off. Von Igelfeld noticed that the white clothes were a uniform of some sort, and that one of them had a small two-way radio with him, which crackled into life as they walked away.

He paused, standing at the edge of the canal, and looked down into the water. It was green and murky, and if one fell in, he thought, well, what then? He remembered reading about a film producer in Rome who had fallen off a houseboat into the Tiber and who had died the next day from swallowing water. Would that happen in Venice? Was the whole city surrounded by poison? And then what was it that the proprietor of the restaurant had said about the sea? Was that poisonous too?

He walked on, but the image of the two men in white stayed in his mind, and he resolved to ask the manager of the hotel all about it if he had the opportunity that evening. Then he could warn the Prinzels about swimming, if need be.

No opportunity presented itself to talk to any of the hotel staff before dinner, so the topic did not come up at the table. The Prinzels had had an exhausting day, with a trip to Murano and several circumnavigations of the city on *vaporetti*. Ophelia had insisted upon a gondola ride, which Prinzel had eventually agreed to, but it had not been a success as the gondolier had apparently deliberately splashed Prinzel with water, or so Prinzel alleged.

'Did it get in your mouth?' von Igelfeld asked anxiously, but Prinzel assured him that it had merely covered his jacket.

'But why do you think it was deliberate?' von Igelfeld asked.

Prinzel's reply came quickly. 'Because he said to me, "Why are you Germans so scared of the water these days?" and then, before I had the chance to ask him what he meant, he splashed me. It was deliberate all right!'

Von Igelfeld caught his breath. This was consistent with what the restaurant proprietor had said to him about the Germans not coming. But why should they be afraid of the water? Nobody had said anything about the sea being dangerous in any way. There were no notices; there was nothing in the newspapers. Certainly the Grand Hôtel des Bains continued to offer its guests beach towels and bathing cabins. If the sea were perilous, then surely no responsible hotel would do that.

Von Igelfeld felt uneasy, but he did not wish to alarm the Prinzels unnecessarily. The following day he was to visit his one friend in Venice, Dottore Reggio Malvestiti, Librarian of the Biblioteca Filologica of the University of Venice. He knew that he could ask him about it and expect an honest answer. And at least Prinzel had not swallowed any water, so they were still safe.

Dottore Reggio Malvestiti, alerted by von Igelfeld's telephone call from the Grand Hôtel des Bains, was waiting for his visitor on the steps of the Biblioteca Filologica, a handsome sixteenth-century palazzo on the Rio dei Santi Apostoli.

'Dear Igelfeld,' he said, moving forward to embrace the great philologist. 'You must come to see us more often. We miss you so!'

Von Igelfeld, always slightly taken aback by Italian emotion-alism, searched for an appropriate response, but found none. He need not have worried, however; Malvestiti immediately drew him into the entrance hall of the library and launched into an impassioned address on the subject of Morati's behaviour at the Siena Conference. Von Igelfeld listened as best he could, nodding agreement from time to time, but unable to make his way through the labyrinths of internecine Italian academic politics. Malevestiti appeared to be reaching the conclusion that Morati had at last lost his reason, and von Igelfeld signalled here his warm assent. He had always found a somewhat manic aspect to Morati's conduct. In the past he had put this down to his being Italian, but perhaps there was more to it than that. Perhaps Malvestiti was right.

They progressed through the entrance hall and made their way along a narrow corridor to Malvestiti's office. There Malvestiti pushed von Igelfeld into a chair (somewhat rudely, von Igelfeld thought) and continued his diatribe against Morati. Von Igelfeld, waiting for a pause, at last managed to interject his question.

'Is there something wrong with Venice?' he asked. 'Please give me a direct answer. That is all I want.'

Malvestiti, about to reveal a further perfidy on Morati's part, was stopped in his tracks.

'Venice?' he asked. 'Something wrong?'

Von Igelfeld nodded. 'Yes, Venice. I have seen men in white coats peering into the canal and taking samples of the water.'

For a few moments Malvestiti appeared to be thinking about this and said nothing. Then he sighed.

'Alas, you are right,' he said quietly. 'There is a great deal wrong with Venice. The water is rising. The city is sinking. Soon we shall all be gone. Even this library . . . ' He stopped, and spread the palms of his hands in a gesture of despair. Then he continued: 'We have already lost an entire floor of this library – our entire Slavonic collection. It is now completely underwater.'

Von Igelfeld drew in his breath sharply. Surely the books themselves could not be submerged. Malvestiti, as if anticipating his question, smiled ruefully.

'Yes,' he said. 'It may seem ridiculous, but we just didn't have the time to save them. Come, let me show you.'

They made their way down further corridors, lit only with weak, bare bulbs. Then, faced with a small panelled door, Malvestiti pushed it open. There was a staircase immediately beyond the door, and this descended sharply into water some two or three feet below.

'There,' said Malvestiti sadly. 'Look at that.'

Von Igelfeld stared down at the water. Malvestiti had taken a torch from the wall and was shining it onto the surface of the water, just below which he could make out the beginnings of a bookshelf and the spines of books.

'I can hardly believe it,' he said. 'Were you unable to do anything to save the books?'

Malvestiti looked down at the water, as if willing it to retreat.

'It happened without our realising it,' he said. 'Very few people ask for those books, and months, even years can go by with nobody going downstairs. Then, suddenly, an Archimandrite working in the library asked for a work on Church Slavonic, and there we were . . . Now, if you see the mark *s.a* on a book's catalogue card, you know it means that it is *sub aqua*. It is very sad.'

That evening von Igelfeld sat on the terrace of the Grand Hôtel des Bains in sombre mood. His mind was on his meeting with Malvestiti

– normally such a warm occasion – this year an encounter which left him filled with nothing but feelings of foreboding. He had realised that his friend had not in fact provided the answers to the real question which he had asked. Everybody knew that Venice was sinking – that was not the point. The real question was what was wrong with the water?

He gazed out at the sea, now becoming dark with the setting of the sun. It looked so beautiful, so maternal, and yet there must be something very wrong with it. Von Igelfeld sipped on his drink, a cold glass of beer, noticing with satisfaction that the label on the bottle said 'Brewed in Belgium'. That must be safe; there was nothing threatening about Belgium. Ineffably dull, perhaps; but not threatening.

Taking a further sip of his beer, von Igelfeld glanced down the terrace. There was hardly a soul about yet, although the terrace would fill up as the evening wore on. People were in their rooms now, showering or bathing; preparing for the civilised delights of the Venetian evening. In a short while, the Prinzels would appear, and they would discuss the events of the day. The prospect made von Igelfeld feel considerably more cheerful. Ophelia, in particular, could always be counted upon to raise the dullest of spirits.

He looked at the tubs of bright flowers, perched on the parapet. How good the Italians were with colours; how bold the reds, how deep the purples, and . . . what was that? Somebody had left something on one of the chairs near the parapet. It looked rather like a camera.

Von Igelfeld looked about to see if there was a waiter whose attention could be drawn to the lost item, but nobody was there. So he got up, strode across to the chair, and lifted up the small instrument. It was a very curious camera, he thought, and very heavy.

The weight made him suspicious, and so his examination continued further. He thought perhaps it was a light meter, as there was a dial across the face of the instrument, and a small hand piece that was presumably pointed in the direction of the light source. But then he saw it, neatly printed beneath the dial: Geiger Counter: Made in Switzerland.

For a moment von Igelfeld stood quite still, his thoughts in turmoil. He was no scientist, but he was well enough informed to know Geiger counters were designed to measure radiation. Who could have left it there, and why? He remembered seeing men in white coats around the hotel just before he came out on the terrace. He had assumed that they were collecting samples of water, but was this what they were doing? The thought appalled him.

Von Igelfeld returned to his table, cradling the Geiger counter in his arms, as if it might explode if he dropped it. He saw that there was an on/off switch and with his heart thumping wildly within him, he turned the switch to the on position. Nothing happened. A light glowed behind the dial, but the needle stayed quite still.

He picked up the handpiece and pointed it down at the ground. Nothing. Then he moved it towards his shoes, and for a moment the needle gave a slight twitch and von Igelfeld thought he heard a click. But the needle went back, and he breathed again. Then, hardly daring to look, he moved the hand piece up over his trouser legs and towards his stomach. Nothing. Nothing except the wild thumping of the heart. Further up, over the breast, face, hair. Nothing.

Von Igelfeld put down the instrument and heaved a sigh of relief. It was ridiculous, he thought. He was imagining the whole thing. People used Geiger counters for all sorts of purposes, he thought, such as . . . He stopped. Was there any other reason to have a Geiger counter?

[123]

'Moritz-Maria! So here you are!'

Ophelia, standing above him, bent down and kissed his brow.

'Well,' said Prinzel, from behind her. 'What sort of day have you had?'

Von Igelfeld smiled as his guests sat down – Ophelia opposite him, Prinzel right next to him. And as Prinzel sat down, the Geiger counter beside him emitted a loud clicking sound.

'What was that?' asked Prinzel. 'Did you want to say something?'

Von Igelfeld was too shocked to speak. Mutely, he pointed at the Geiger counter.

'What's that?' asked Prinzel. 'Is that some sort of radio?'

'A Geiger counter,' von Igelfeld stuttered.

'Ah,' said Prinzel. 'How useful! Let me test myself!'

With an awful sense of his own inability to prevent the occurrence of a tragedy, von Igelfeld watched as Prinzel turned the hand piece towards himself and ran it down his body. Once again the instrument clicked, and the needle jerked on the dial.

'Mmm,' said Prinzel, peering at the dial. 'A bit of a reaction. Not too bad.'

Von Igelfeld gasped. 'You mean . . . '

'Yes,' said Prinzel calmly. 'I seem to have picked something up. Probably something I ate.'

Von Igelfeld protested lamely. 'But that's awful,' he said. 'Radioactivity is terribly dangerous.'

'Yes,' agreed Prinzel. 'I think I had probably better go and seek treatment at home. They'll give me iodine pills or something.' He looked across the table at Ophelia, who was smiling benignly. She clearly knew little about radioactivity.

'I shan't be upset to be going home early,' she said. 'Venice is still so hot . . . '

For von Igelfeld, an early departure could not be early enough. He had found out what was wrong with the city, and he was horrified. It was worse than plague; it was worse than cholera. It was almost too awful to contemplate.

They finished their drinks quietly, and then processed into the great dining hall. Von Igelfeld took the Geiger counter with him, determined to run it over each course before they ate it, and this he did discreetly, hoping not to attract the attention of the waiters. The paté was quite all right, as was the salad, but the fish sent the needle shooting to the top of the scale, and it was dispatched back to the kitchen, with no explanation.

Then the band struck up, playing one of those infectiously gay Italian country tunes. Couples began to dance, and Prinzel and Ophelia, with von Igelfeld's blessing, left the table, and were soon out on the dance floor. Von Igelfeld stayed where he was, and was sitting with the Geiger counter on his lap as the Polish boy, in a fresh white sailor suit, glowing with health, walked slowly past him, and threw him a glance as he did so.

Von Igelfeld's puzzled irritation was matched only by his surprise. As the boy walked past, the Geiger counter clicked hysterically and the needle shot up to the very reddest part of the scale. Von Igelfeld's mouth opened in an astonishment that was quickly followed by dismay. He must have been swimming. That was it! Poor youth!

He looked about him. The boy had now joined his mother and sisters at their table and their meal was being ordered. Oh what tragedy! thought von Igelfeld. And so young too! It was as if the very floor of the Grand Hôtel des Bains was littered with fallen rose petals and abandoned mandolins.

For a few minutes he wrestled with conflicting emotions. He assumed that there was nothing he could really do at this stage to help the unfortunate youth. It was none of his business, really, or was it? Was he his neighbour's keeper, even when his neighbour was a rather strange Polish boy who kept looking at him in a disconcerting fashion? Yes, he was, he decided. He must warn the mother – that's what he must do.

Von Igelfeld arose from his table, straightened his tie, and walked over to the Polish family's table. As he approached, the mother raised her eyes, and smiled at him.

'*Excusez-moi, Madame,*' said von Igelfeld. '*Permettez-moi de vous dire que votre fils, votre très agréable Tadseuz, est devenu un peu radio-actif.*'

The mother listened, and inclined her head gravely at the information.

'*Merci, monsieur,*' she said after a short pause. '*Vous êtes très gentil de me donner ces informations. Je vous remercie bien. J'ai*

*des convictions bien intensives au sujet de la radio-activité parmi
les enfants.'*

Von Igelfeld waited for something further to be said, but it was
not, and so he bowed, and returned to his table, where the Prinzels
were now waiting. They passed the Geiger counter over their
coffee, to negative results, and enjoyed the rest of the evening as one
might enjoy an evening which was to be one's last in Venice, ever.

It might have been a melancholy departure the next day, but as
they made their farewells to the manager, who expressed great
regret on their premature departure, a telegram arrived addressed
to von Igelfeld. He opened it with all the sense of foreboding with
which one opens telegrams when away from home, but his face lit
up as he read the message.

MEDAL AWARDED BY PORTUGUESE GOVERNMENT,

the telegram ran.

QUITE DELIGHTED. BEST WISHES, UNTERHOLZER.

Von Igelfeld thrust the telegram into Ophelia's hands and turned
to Prinzel.

'Prinzel,' he said, the dignity in his voice overlaying the emotion.
'I have been honoured by the Portuguese Government – at last!'

They left in the hotel's motor launch, riding over the lagoon to the
fatal, exquisite, doomed city, and then on to the mainland. Thereafter they made their way slowly through the mountains and into
Austria. Throughout the journey von Igelfeld was in a state of
complete euphoria. What would his medal look like? By whom
would it be awarded, and what would be said at the ceremony?
There were so many questions to be answered.

Then, as they passed through a tiny village, with a minute, whitewashed church, Prinzel suddenly turned round and made an observation.

'That telegram,' he said. 'It's just occurred to me that Unterholzer didn't say they'd awarded the medal to you. The wording suggests that it was really to him.'

'What do you mean?' said von Igelfeld angrily. 'He said quite clearly: Medal awarded by Portuguese Government. Quite delighted . . . ' He broke off, becoming silent; could it be . . . ?

They had passed out of the village now, and there was a long, steep mountain pass ahead. Von Igelfeld sat in silence, unable to speak. *Oh!* he thought. And then, *Oh!* again. *Why have I had such bad luck in this life? Why? All I want is love, and a tiny bit of recognition from the Portuguese, and I get neither. And soon it will be too late; nobody will read my book any more, and there will be nobody to remember me.*

He brought himself to order. There was no point in self-pity, which was something he invariably disliked in others. No; he would not allow himself to be discouraged. He had much to be proud of in this life; much for which he should be grateful. He was, after all, Professor Dr Moritz-Maria von Igelfeld. That, on its own, would have been quite enough; but there was more: he was the author of *Portuguese Irregular Verbs*, and that was something that would forever be associated with his name, just as when people thought of Thomas Mann they thought of . . .

Von Igelfeld stopped. And then he laughed, which made Prinzel swerve the car slightly before he righted it and they continued their journey back to Germany, where they belonged.